The Book of Kills

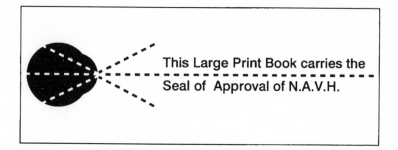

THE
BOOK
OF KILLS

A Mystery Set at the
University of Notre Dame

Ralph McInerny

Thorndike Press • Waterville, Maine

Published in 2001 by arrangement with
St. Martin's Press, LLC.

Thorndike Press Large Print Basic Series.

The tree indicium is a trademark of Thorndike Press.

The text of this Large Print edition is unabridged.
Other aspects of the book may vary from the original edition.

Set in 16 pt. Plantin by Rick Gundberg.

Printed in the United States on permanent paper.

Library of Congress Cataloging-in-Publication Data

McInerny, Ralph M.
   The book of kills : a mystery set at the University of
Notre Dame / Ralph McInerny.
      p.   cm.
   ISBN 0-7862-3642-6 (lg. print : hc : alk. paper)
   1. University of Notre Dame — Fiction. 2. Indian land
transfers — Fiction. 3. South Bend (Ind.) — Fiction.
4. College teachers — Fiction. 5. Brothers — Fiction.
6. Large type books. I. Title.
PS3563.A31166 B66 2001
                                                      2001048024

To Father Jim Riehle

PROLOGUE

There is a willow grows aslant Saint Mary's lake on its northwestern shore where the path passes beneath Fatima Retreat House. An elderly figure sat on a bench beside the path surrounded by ducks, to whom he was doling out bits of bread. The ducks were always indiscriminate in waddling toward dispensers of food but this morning, after a first unseasonable snowfall, they would willingly have been fed by a butcher. But the old priest ignored that, preferring to think of himself as Saint Francis, who could charm the birds from the trees and talk to animals in their own language.

"Venite ad me omnes," he murmured, on the chance these ducks spoke Latin.

There was a lesson to be learned from the mindless greed with which the ducks responded to sense appetite. Only man must subsume his natural desire for food and drink under the governance of reason. It was a lesson Father James had taught in a lesser college of the Congregation for years, but of late he had been assigned to Fatima Retreat

7

House as a preacher of retreats.

Mid-October was a slack time for retreats, and the snow brought thoughts of Christmas and the weeks when the house would be empty and he need think only of his own soul. The creche would remain in chapel long after Epiphany and the smell of pine would perfume his prayers. And, of course, the students would be gone on vacation and the campus, too, all but empty. But this morning's snow was already beginning to melt and soon autumn would be back in full force.

When the bread was gone, the ducks continued to crowd around. He showed them that the bag was empty but they remained. He had neglected to say grace on their behalf before feeding them and said it now.

"Benedic nos, domine, et haec tua dona . . ."

The ducks began to go quacking off to the lake. Perhaps they spoke French or Italian. The priest flattened and folded the empty bag and put it into the pocket of his coat. He rose from the bench. It was time for exercise. He started along the path in a westerly direction, moving slowly. He did not really believe in exercise. Exercise was a poor substitute for genuine labor in a generation gone soft with luxury. He smiled away the thought. He was Francis not Jeremiah.

This thought was reenforced when half a

dozen ducks accompanied him along the path. Clearly they were not land animals, only imperfectly amphibian. But their pace suited his. He was in no hurry. From time to time he stopped and looked back the way he had come, at the spire of Sacred Heart, at the great golden dome of the Main Building. Once, Father Sorin's eyes had rested on them. He felt a profound solidarity with the founder of the Congregation in which he had labored for some forty years.

When he turned he found that his escort of ducks had continued up the path. One had wandered from it and was seeking to conceal what it had found. But the other ducks were not deceived. They waddled across the snow and soon there was a quacking contest for the prize. Father James wondered vaguely what it could be? What foodstuff could they have come upon?

When he reached the point on the path from which they had set off to the quarrel, he stopped again to look benignly at his feathered friends. What they were fighting over seemed feathered, too. His curiosity, usually dormant, was piqued. He went across the snow and found that they were playing tug of war with what looked like an Indian headdress. And then he saw the body.

The man was all but covered with snow and

there were now many duck tracks around the body. Father James hurried forward and knelt before saying the formula of absolution over the man. Who knew how long the soul would take to leave a frozen body? The back of the head was exposed now that the headdress had been removed. Masses of blood had blackened and frozen in the matted hair. Father James struggled to his feet and as he returned to the path he shooed the ducks before him. Stupid beasts.

And then he went on, in what an undemanding observer might have described as a jog, back to the house to spread the alarm.

1

The trouble began on an October Saturday at the log chapel.

Two stretch limos came up the road behind Bond Hall, which housed the architecture department, and parked. Out of them poured a wedding party. The bride wore a traditional white gown, the bridesmaids were in blue, the men in formal attire. The groom was an alumnus, the bride his childhood sweetheart, and he was fulfilling an undergraduate dream of being married in the log chapel on the Notre Dame campus, a venue in even more demand than Sacred Heart Basilica, the university church. Father Burnside, who had been rector of the groom's undergraduate dorm, was to meet them at the chapel door.

But there was no sign of the priest.

The chapel door was guarded by two men done up in traditional Indian garb.

"Have you seen a priest?"

"He's inside."

They did not get out of the way. The best man, another alumnus, had made the football team as a student, a tight end who had played a total of eight minutes in a game that had been won already in the first half. He stepped forward, expanded his chest, and explained that a wedding was scheduled.

"The priest is our prisoner," one of the Native Americans said. "We are reclaiming our property."

In Cedar Grove Cemetery, the sexton was appalled, the more so because he had not noticed the outrage when he came to work that morning, though he must have driven right past the toppled grave markers. One had stood six feet tall and when it fell had done damage to a number of neighboring graves. The sexton called for his crew to make a thorough reconnaissance to see if there were other instances of vandalism.

He assumed that it *was* vandalism, kids from town in the momentary grip of adolescent madness who had thought pushing over gravestones made some profound statement to the universe. There were three desecrated graves, if that was not too heightened a way of putting it. The sexton did not think so. He used the term five times in speaking to campus security. To the provost he spoke of sacrilege.

Cedar Grove Cemetery was as old as the university itself. It was located on Notre

Dame Avenue, as good as on the campus, just south of the bookstore and Eck Alumni Center. For some years there had not been a single unspoken-for grave site in Cedar Grove, but more land had been acquired to the west when the golf course was relocated and now a fortunate few more could look forward to awaiting the last trump in the company of the earliest generation of South Bend.

It was Roger Knight, the Huneker Professor of Catholic Studies, who later noticed a pattern in the vandalism.

Coquillard, Pokagon, Pokagon's son.

Old Father Carmody nodded. "Contemporaries of Father Sorin." Edward Sorin was the founder of the University of Notre Dame, a visionary French priest of the Congregation of Holy Cross who had found a small trading community on a bend in the Saint Joseph River when he came to claim the property he had bought for what he grandly called his university. "Frenchmen like himself," Carmody added.

"Not entirely, Father. Some of them had Indian blood as well. And Pokagon was a chief."

Meanwhile, Father Burnside had been released from custody and the wedding in the log chapel went on as planned. But when the happy couple and their party returned to their rented vehicles to be driven away to the Morris Inn for the reception they had to pass between ragged rows of half a dozen surly men all dressed up as Indians.

"What's going on?"

"Keno sabe?"

"Be careful."

On the following day, Wednesday, the university chancellor did not return as scheduled from a trip to Hong Kong. A call to the Michiana Airport revealed that he had arrived in South Bend on the appropriate flight.

"Johnny!" said Miss Trafficant impatiently. Anita Trafficant was the chancellor's secretary and Johnny the chancellor's driver. There was enmity between her and Johnny. The chauffeur had an annoying habit of acting as if he worked directly for the chancellor and was on an equal footing with Miss Trafficant! She would not have been human if she did not relish the thought of scolding him for whatever had happened. But he did not answer his car phone.

Miss Trafficant believed in scheduling. Her success at her job depended in large part on the efficient way in which she arranged the chancellor's day. Without her precise allocation of his time, he could not have done half of what he did. She had allowed an hour and a half from the time of his arrival at the airport to the first appointment of the day. Father Bloom should be well rested from his long flight in business class across the Pacific.

Two hours passed and the chancellor had not arrived on campus or come to his office. The tenth call to Johnny's car got an answer. His speech was slurred and he made little sense.

"Have you been drinking?"

The answering obscenity was sufficiently garbled that she could honorably ignore it. She managed to learn where he was.

"You were supposed to pick up Father."

There was a call on her other phone. She cut off Johnny and took the call.

"This is the Blue Cloud Nation. The chancellor of Notre Dame is our prisoner. Stand by for further instructions."

The phone went dead.

The consensus in the lounge of Corby, the building where lived priests who were not rectors of residence halls, was that it was a student prank. Johnny had been slipped a mickey and the students who met the chancellor's plane hit upon the politically incorrect excuse that Indians had kidnapped him in an effort to reclaim the property on which the university stood. True, this theory had been floated recently in an allegedly humorous column in the student newspaper, but then it was difficult to distinguish intended from unintended humor in that publication.

"They got the idea from the log chapel incident."

"Or the vandalism in Cedar Grove."

"What if they're all connected?"

"How?"

The speaker had held up one hand as he spoke, but then immediately let it drop to the arm of his chair.

In the faculty senate the Quinlan Resolution was being debated. If passed, it would become the sense of the senate that the administration should appoint a committee to meet with the Blue Cloud Nation in order to review with utmost seriousness their claim that ancestors had been bilked out of the land on which Notre Dame stood.

"It doesn't matter," one phlegmatic senator observed. "There isn't a patch of earth that was not at one time inhabited by someone other than those currently inhabiting it."

"These people weren't even alive at the time."

"Their quarrel is with Sorin."

"He's dead."

"So are their ancestors."

"It's a matter of justice."

"You want to give the place back to the Indians?"

"If they'll have it."

"If it is theirs it would not be a gift."

An observer from the *Observer* thought that the senate as a body was inclined to think that Notre Dame had been built on a foundation of injustice and crime.

A video of the captive chancellor was delivered to Corby Hall. He looked disheveled and unfocused, but then he wasn't wearing his glasses. He seemed to be reciting when he spoke.

"I have pledged to correct any injustice that has been done against the Blue Cloud Nation by the University of Notre Dame."

His eyes lifted to the camera and filled with tears. His lower lip trembled. "I'm sorry," he said.

"He didn't know what he was saying."

"So what's new?"

"He was just reading words written for him."

"So what's new?"

"You can't just wish away an institution that has been situated on this land for over a century and a half. What would the Indians do with the land?"

"A casino?"

"They'd sell it."

"That's the answer! Give it back to them and then we buy it right back. If all they want is money . . ."

This turned out not to be true. They wanted the land. They wanted the lakes. They wanted the woodland. They wanted their old burial ground back.

"Where is it?"

"It has yet to be located."

2

In a conference room in Decio a few days before the trouble began, the graduate committee of the history department was in session. The first order of business was the fate of Orion Plant, a doctoral candidate.

"We've already extended him two times."

"Who's his director?"

Professor Otto Ranke raised his hand but not his eyes. He had lied for Plant too many times and he was not inclined to do so again. The inevitable question was asked.

"Has he made progress on his dissertation?"

"No."

"Is there any reason why the rule should not be applied?" The rule was that a doctoral candidate must submit his dissertation for reading and defense within seven years of getting approval of his topic. Plant's dissertation had been approved eleven years ago. Ranke was not only the director, he was the only survivor of the original committee. All the others were retired or dead. Or both.

"The rule should have been applied earlier."

A vote was taken. The decision was unanimous. Sencil, the director of graduate studies, said he would convey the decision to Plant, but Ranke said that task must be his. The others might rightly feel that they had condemned someone in absentia. Had they even known Plant? Ranke felt that he had just bade adieu to his golden years. Plant was the last candidate who had sought to do a dissertation under his direction.

"What was the topic anyway?"

"The relocation of Indians to the southwest."

The love of learning takes many forms. In some, it is a pure gemlike flame that warms and does not consume the student. In others, it is a means to ameliorate the human condition, first of all in their own case. In a few, as for Nietzsche, it is a path to power for whom knowledge becomes a weapon. A blunt weapon in the case of science, a remote and transcendental one in the case of philosophy, but subtle and sure in the case of history. From the outset, Orion Plant had seen history as revenge upon the present.

As a boy in Toledo he had spent hot summer afternoons in the attic of his grandmother's home, turning over the pages of old albums and ledgers, pondering the facts entered on the flyleaves of old family bibles. He was fascinated, a question grew in him, he followed the spoor of possibility. It was there in the attic with lungs filled with dusty air and sweat running down his broad freckled face, that he had discovered he was not his parents' child. His family was not his family. He had not even been legally adopted. His apparent parents had taken him in when a neighbor went on a trip. The neighbor never returned. With time, the family gave Orion their name and neglected to tell him he was not one of their own. After a moment of vertigo and a pang of sadness, Orion found the discovery oddly exhilarating. What he would learn to call research was a means of overturning the apparently real world.

Acquiring the academic credentials to pursue the surprising secrets of the recorded past as a lifetime task turned out to be more demanding and less interesting than Orion had supposed. But he persisted. He got an undergraduate degree at a small college in his native state and was then admitted to graduate studies at the University of Notre Dame. When he left Toledo he metaphorically shook its dust from his sandals. At Notre Dame he took with diminishing interest the required number of courses. Availing himself of the unofficial archives kept by generations of graduate students in history, he passed the written and oral examinations and was admitted as a candidate for the doctorate. Resentfully prowling through the past of the area, he chose a topic and it was approved. Professor Ranke nodded sagely through clouds of the sweet smoke rising from his pipe. Orion would chronicle the forced march of local Indians to Kansas just prior to the founding of Notre Dame. He would focus on the martyred devotion of Father Petit, who had accompanied the Indians on their death march. The benign official version of the transfer of the land to Father Sorin invited skepticism.

"He's buried in the crypt of Sacred Heart." Ranke sent up his words in little puffs of smoke. Orion looked at his director impassively. He had nodded through the professor's boring lectures, but now his estimate of his guide sank further. Orion had found the burial plot of Father Edward Sorin in the community cemetery located just off the road that led from the grotto to the highway across which stood Saint Mary's College, the sister institution of Notre Dame.

"Father Sorin?" The question was meant to make Ranke's ignorance explicit.

"No, no. Petit."

"Ah."

Orion thought Ranke might be wrong at

least in this, but he was not. This oddly increased his disguised contempt for his director. He began his research.

He had been at it three years when he met Marcia. She worked in the Huddle, preparing stir-fried concoctions to order. He might not have noticed her if she had not, surreptitiously but making sure he noticed, put a double portion of chicken in his order as she began to cook it. The second time this happened he read the name on the plastic badge she wore.

"Marcia."

"Marcia Younger."

"Than what?"

Her pained expression told him he was not the first to make a bad joke of her name.

"I'm sorry."

"Everybody does it."

"I'm Orion Plant."

"I know."

Those behind him in the line were beginning to mutter, but Marcia was practiced in antagonizing customers. He pushed on, paid, and took a table. Some minutes later, minus the plastic snood she wore over her hair while stir-frying, Marcia joined him.

"I asked who you were, that's how I know."

And so it began. She was a substantial young woman but her face was pretty, made even prettier by the adoring expression in her eyes. He was not used to the deference she showed him. She had the impression that he was a junior member of the faculty. As a graduate assistant, he was part of the platoon of indentured servants who made life even easier for the faculty. He felt that he was monitoring the professor's lectures and in his discussion sessions he subtly corrected what Ranke had said. He did not correct Marcia's misapprehension. After all, in a few years . . .

Her father was dead, her mother stone deaf; Orion became a constant visitor in their small house just east of the campus, within walking distance of graduate student housing on Bulla Road. As they walked back from her house they could see Hesburgh Library lift like a great sarcophagus among the trees. It was there that his study carrel was located. After a few months, they seemed to be engaged. When, given her passionate yielding, an early marriage seemed advisable, Orion told her they would be married in the log chapel.

"I'm not Catholic."

"That doesn't matter." In his cluttered, imperfectly formed Catholic mind a cunning thought occurred. Marriage to Marcia might not really count so far as the great book in the sky was concerned. He changed his mind about the log chapel, citing as reason his great reluctance that he might be married among those primitive paintings in which the natives obsequiously received the great white fathers. Orion and Marcia were married in the court-house by a judge who had just sentenced a man to life imprisonment. Orion did not voice the joke that occurred to him. They honeymooned in Niles and moved in with her mother. Marcia wrote down the good news for her mother to read after several shouted versions failed to get through to her staring, open-mouthed parent.

Her father had been in real estate as had his father before him, the family business going back generations. The records of the now-defunct enterprise were in old wooden file cabinets stored in a rental locker north of town. An hour spent perusing them piqued his interest and Orion brought the records to the house and it was not long before his pas-sion for research was diverted to the records of Younger Real Estate. The records went back into the nineteenth century and proved to be a vein of precious ore.

3

When Roger Knight had accepted the offer of the Huneker Chair of Catholic studies, his brother Philip, a private detective, moved to South Bend with him. For Roger, Notre Dame might be second only to Bardstown, Kentucky, in the American past of the church to which he had converted while a precocious graduate student at Princeton, but for Philip it was a place where seasons of sports succeeded one another liturgically. He continued to conduct his business, though more and more sporadically, from their new location. Roger had earned his doctorate *summa cum laude* at the age of nineteen, a boy who had inflated to dirigible size in the course of his accelerated studies. Armed with his degree he had emerged into a professional world that eyed him with wary caution. He had been on the short list for several teaching positions but in the end was given, in Philip's phrase, the short end of the stick. He lost interest in poring over *The Chronicle of Higher Education* for other opportunities and eventually, when Philip retreated from his

Manhattan location to the comparative civility of Rye, Roger applied for and received a private investigator's license and Philip's advertisement in the Yellow Pages of strategically chosen major cities announced that Knight Brothers Investigations could be reached at the 800 number listed. Roger created a Web page as well and for some years they had taken on clients with a problem interesting enough to lure them from Rye. Meanwhile, Roger read and communicated via e-mail with kindred spirits about the globe on the myriad of things that engaged his scholarly mind. He wrote a book on Frederick Rolfe, aka Baron Corvo, which enjoyed first a *succès d'estime* and then, thanks to its selection by the History Book Club and its adoption by Barnes and Noble, enjoyed a wide readership as well. It was this book that caught the attention of Father Carmody and led to the offer of the Huneker chair.

At Notre Dame, Roger was a free variable floating over departmental divisions. He taught but one course a semester and it was cross-listed in English, philosophy, theology, and history. It was thanks to the latter connection that he had come to know Otto Ranke, an elderly professor to whom the concept of retirement was anathema. To Roger he represented a Notre Dame that was no more, a remnant of the small band whose teaching and writing bore the stamp of the religious affiliation of the university. Now Notre Dame described itself as a national research university and its distinctiveness as an institution, academically at least, was threatened. Today, Otto Ranke, with his interests in the role of the American bishops at Vatican II, and a monograph on distinguished visitors to the South Bend campus that had featured F. Marion Crawford, Robert Hugh Benson, Henry James, and William Butler Yeats, would have been an unlikely prospect for a position in the history department. With the retirement of Marvin O'Connell and Philip Gleason, Ranke was the history department for Roger Knight.

"A student of mine is writing his dissertation on that," Ranke said one day when they were discussing the past of the coordinates of space the university occupied, and the fate of the Indians had come up.

"I'd like to meet him."

"No, you wouldn't."

"Why?"

"An odd fellow."

Roger would have thought this would be a commendation rather than the reverse for Professor Ranke, but no further explanation was offered. They sat for a moment in silence, enveloped in the smoke from Otto's pipe. The smoke, from irresistible sweetness turned over time into something approaching the American pronunciation of the professor's family name, and there were complaints from purists along the corridor of Decio Hall. Notre Dame was listed as a smoke-free campus, something that Ranke considered the result of the guttering of the fire of proud and confident Catholicity among the faculty. But he had been here before most of the campus buildings went up, his colleagues' parents had been children when he joined the faculty, and he was unmoved by their reiterated complaints. Smoking was still grudgingly permitted in the faculty office building, but plaintiffs insisted that cigars and pipes were excluded. They had no case. If Ranke noticed that he had been ostracized as an inconsiderate old bastard devoid of sensitivity, he gave no sign of it, but serenely lighted pipe full after pipe full of his aromatic offering to a better day.

Their conversation turned to the recent events in Cedar Grove Cemetery. Ranke nodded as if it too were an expected consequence of the university's swerve into secularization.

"Bigots," he opined, and began to speak of past episodes, notably the depredations of the KKK.

"Religion doesn't seem to be at the bottom if it," Roger said.

"Religion is at the bottom of everything."

Nothing could have stated more succinctly Roger's own conviction and he settled back contentedly to Ranke's impromptu lecture on the hooded hordes that had once harassed the campus.

4

In his opulent office in the recently renovated Main Building, the chancellor brooded. Memories of the men who had met his plane when he returned from Hong Kong made him feel vulnerable to unknown menaces. His bags had been commandeered and he had been ushered swiftly to an exit.

"Where's Johnny?"

The answer was lost in the racket made by the automatic doors of the terminal. Outside, an unseasonable cold greeted him. Father Bloom was pulling up the collar of his coat when his elbows were seized by the two accompanying him and he was hustled into a waiting car that was definitely not the university vehicle that was Johnny's pride. The driver behind the wheel was not Johnny. The car had sped off, the chancellor was unceremoniously conked on the head, and a darkness almost welcome after his long journey descended.

When consciousness returned he found himself in a small unlit room. There was a single television camera standing straddle-legged in a corner.

"You awake?" The voice might have been one of those that had come to Joan of Arc except for its cryptic menace.

"Where am I?"

"In custody."

Silence. His further questions went unanswered. He realized that he was bound to the chair in which he sat with rope pulled tightly about legs and chest and knotted firmly. Fear rose in Father Bloom's breast. In foreign lands, he was often warned about the risk of physical dangers due to local political conditions. He had never thought of South Bend as similarly threatening. His aprehension took the form of a Stevensonian title. *Kidnapped.* It had been one of his favorite books as a boy; he had dreamed of going into literature, but he had been ordered into theology where he had languished until he was plucked from the ranks and groomed for the soon-to-be-created office of chancellor of the university. From then on he had been the toy of one éminence grise after another, shadowy figures he had never thought of as forces in the Congregation. They had great plans for the forward leap of the university. He led a charge that others had planned. Where were his mentors now when his life was threatened?

Not a day had passed before he was marching to the drum of his unseen oppressors. The television camera was turned on from another room and he spoke the words he had memorized. When at the end he blurted out, "I'm sorry," his act of contrition might have covered sins undreamed of by those who held him captive.

On the second day, after hours when no bodiless commands or questions had come to him as if from airy spirits, the door was opened and his rescuers appeared. They had been informed by telephone where he could be found. He babbled half coherently of his ordeal.

"A prank," he was told.

"A prank!"

"The less we make of it, the less their triumph will be. A jokester ignored is a sorry sight."

No sorrier sight than the chancellor when he was unbound. He stood, a wobbling Prometheus, and refused the suggestion that he had been the victim of a practical joke.

"They filmed me," he cried. "They made me say things . . ."

"We heard."

"Well?"

"Benign neglect, that's the ticket."

"They were not benign."

"We must be."

Alone now at his desk, he shuddered at the

memories. He had become used to his cere-
monial existence. He was treated with deference wherever he went — except perhaps
during his periodic appearances before the
faculty senate which was dominated by notorious cranks whose careers were not going
well. He was praised and catered to in a way
he wanted to think was not solely due to the
office he held. But his recent ignominy had
been wholly impersonal, his captors had not
cared a whit for him. It was the head of this
great institution, whoever he might be, they
had wanted to humiliate. He still was unable
to gauge the seriousness of their demands.
His advisors must be correct; it had been, in
however bad taste, a prank.

His phone lit up and he answered it to be
told that the university counsel was on the
line.

"I'll speak to him."

"Father," said a fruity voice, "there is
something we must discuss."

"Yes."

"The rogues who detained you have now
retained a lawyer. I have received a communication I don't think can be ignored."

"Come at once."

He put down the phone and once more his
heart sank. It sank further when he learned
that what one of his mentors had jocularly re-

ferred to as the alleged native uprising had secured the services of Bartholomew Leone, a frequent adder at the institutional bosom. Leone had represented disgruntled employees, unpromoted faculty who had decided to sue, a disenchanted assistant coach who had aired dirty athletic laundry in an attempt to recover his position. The chancellor, a teetotaler, suddenly understood the urge some men felt to drink.

5

Orion Plant answered Professor Ranke's summons with foreboding. They discussed his parlous condition as a candidate for a degree and Ranke had not been, as so often in the past he had been, encouraging.

"You have exceeded the allowed limit by four years."

"You know that I am at work on my dissertation."

"I know nothing of the kind. The last time you showed me what you considered the draft of a chapter was half a dozen years ago."

"But I have kept you au courant."

"You have sat there and described at length what you were about to do, but you have not done it."

"Do you have to smoke?"

"It is a pleasure not a necessity. Would you like to step outside for a moment to catch a breath of fresh air?"

"My research has led me in a surprising direction." Plant hitched forward in his chair, his small eyes bright. "Do you know how the natives of this region were robbed by the white man?"

"Orion, the whole country sits on land that could be described as stolen."

"But this is worse."

"Tell me."

Ranke seemed relieved to be deflected from the reason for this interview. His manner at the beginning of the account was skeptical, but as Orion went on he grew impatient.

"You are giving a very slanted version of those events. In any case, Father Badin bought the land from the government which had obtained it by treaty with the Potowatomies. Father Sorin was given the land by the diocese to whom Badin had ceded title."

"Stolen property. That it was paid for does not alter the crime."

"A crime requires the transgression of some law. What statute do you have in mind?"

"Law! Law is the edict of usurpers. I appeal to the natural law, common morality."

"I wonder what a court would make of that."

"I intend to find out."

Ranke was embarrassed by his passion, but Plant was not deterred. He was rehearsing the plea he intended to make before the world, one that had been prepared for by recent events in which he'd had a hand. Around him he had gathered a small band made up of dissidents, other students who found academe mendacious, its requirements unfairly onerous, a make-believe world constructed when the truth was left behind. But mention of the law concentrated Orion's mind. It was soon displaced by what Professor Ranke then told him.

"As far as I know you are not a descendant of the tribe for whom you presume to speak. And as of now you no longer have status in this university. You are no longer a candidate for a degree. I have intervened for you again and again, rules have been bent out of shape for you, and to no avail. Obviously you have been wasting your time on this pointless crusade rather than doing what you are ostensibly here to do. The department long since lost patience with you. I can no longer misrepresent the status of your research. A vote was taken. You have been stricken from the rolls. I asked you here to tell you that."

"Can they do that?"

"They can and they have. And the vote was unanimous."

"You too?" He searched for the phrase and then had it. *"Et tu?"*

"Etiam ego."

What the hell did that mean? But the meaning was unequivocal. His career as a graduate student was over. He felt an odd elation as he rose to his feet.

"Maybe I will consult a lawyer."

"You have no grievance."

"We'll see about that." At the door he turned. It was the moment for a dramatic gesture. But nothing ringing occurred to him. "You haven't seen the last of me," he cried, and left.

The hallway outside, so familiar to him from long years of coming along it to Ranke's office, seemed alien and he an intruder. He could imagine one of the ridiculous members of campus security appearing to take him to the campus entrance and like the angel in Genesis ordering him out of Eden. A muffled cry rose in his throat and his eyes misted with tears. A moment later, eyes brushed dry, he hurried down the corridor, a man with a mission. His pace slowed when he thought of giving this news to Marcia. He had been cashiered, dismissed, fired. Lord, to whom should he go? In the event he went to the only local lawyer whose name was known to him.

6

Bartholomew Leone was a graduate of the Notre Dame law school whose fate it seemingly was to represent those who had some grievance against his alma mater. He had been taught that each has a sacred right to legal representation and he had first assailed his alma mater on a principle she had taught him. But the slings and arrows of previous encounters with the university counsel had turned reluctance to relish and he was in principle disposed to lend a receptive ear to the fanciful claims of Orion Plant.

"Are you a member of the tribe?"

"I could be."

"Don't you know?"

"It doesn't matter."

"You must have status in order to bring such a suit."

"It is a class action."

That surely would be denied by the campus powers that be. Class was one thing Plant surely lacked. He was a pudgy, drab young man whose mouth had acquired the fixed look of one about to whine. In Leone's legal mind, two sidled up to two, separated only by a plus that led inevitably on to four.

"Did you have anything to do with the recent shenanigans on campus?"

Plant adopted a sly look. "Is this conversation confidential?"

"Not if you mean to tell me of felonies you have committed. Desecrating a cemetery, upsetting a wedding, taking two priests into custody."

"Two?"

"Father Burnside and the chancellor."

Truth became a weapon, not an absolute. The common morality to which Plant had appealed in speaking to Professor Ranke seemed foreign to this law office. He had the vague notion that if he were frank with Leone, the lawyer would swiftly turn on him and he would be in real trouble. Locking Burnside in the log chapel was arguably a nuisance, but with the chancellor a charge of kidnapping could be brought. The small engine of graduate school regulations had crushed him. He did not mean to submit himself to the harsher machinery of the law.

"No."

"You had nothing to do with all that?"

"Those events served as catalyst. They dovetailed with my research. Suddenly my path was clear."

One can doubt a client's word without accusing him of lying. Leone asked himself if his doubts of the truth of what Plant said rose to the level of conviction. His mind was suddenly dazzled by the prospect of shaking the university to its very foundations. He imagined a prone university counsel, his neck under the Leone foot.

"Tell me about your research."

Listening, Leone thought of other nuts he had represented against the university, but Plant was an original. Someone who had been denied tenure might rant about academic standards, fairness, the benighted members of his department's committee, but in the end it was a personal vendetta. If the iniquitous decision could not be reversed, the victim intended to go down with all guns blasting. *Après moi le déluge,* that sort of thing. At best Leone could achieve some monetary settlement in exchange for their agreement to go silently. Utter confidentiality about the deal struck was a condition of any money changing hands.

"Here's your thirty pieces of silver," Ballast, the university counsel, would say, handing over a check for the agreed-on amount, holding it by the corner as if to avoid being sullied by such tainted money.

"I had a difficult time," Leone would say.

"It could easily have gone to court."

"But your client talked you out of it."

Ballast was short and overweight and he wore three-piece suits as if they were a uniform of his position. The coats hung long on him, the buttons bulged with his well-fed torso, the tips of his shoes were just visible beneath the cuffs of his trousers. Leone sometimes dreamed of battling with this effete clown before a jury. He would wear a corduroy jacket, a knit tie, khaki trousers. The forces of the proletariat against well-dressed entrenched wealth. For all his shown reluctance in handing over the check, Leone knew that the counsel was relieved to have kept the quarrel out of the courts and the details of the settlement from the newspapers.

Orion Plant presented a challenge. His charges were so fanciful that not even his silence might induce the university to turn over any cash to the recently released graduate student. Leone would have been happy to pursue the difficult task of proving that Plant had been unfairly treated, despite his undeniable failure to meet the minimal standards of the time allotted to completing a dissertation. There was always something that could be turned into a plus for a client. For all its regulations, academia was a place where the whimsical ruled. He would hale members of

43

the graduate committee before the court, he would examine their own credentials and experience as graduate students in minute detail. Something would turn up, something always did. And when it did, Leone would know what to do with it. Within weeks he would be in negotiations with the university counsel. But Orion Plant's complaint had the taint of the altruistic, and Leone listened to his potential client unconvinced.

Leone had been raised on westerns and was ill disposed to consider Native Americans as sympathetic. A brother-in-law had recently cashed in his retirement and lost the entire amount to a casino run by a Wisconsin tribe. There ought to be a law against letting an idiot like his brother-in-law gamble away the security he had amassed over a lifetime. Leone was on the side of the sheriff, the posse, the lone platoon setting out from the fort into Apache country. Orion Plant was asking him to see those forces of civilization as exploiters. He looked at his watch.

"What do you think?" Plant asked.

"You don't have a chance."

"You haven't been listening."

"The problem is that I have."

"Let me leave this with you."

"This" was a manuscript bound at Kinko's. The cover read: *The Case Against Notre Dame:*

A House Built Upon a Stolen Sand. Leone said he would read it. Somewhat to his surprise, he did.

He read it late into the night, sipping scotch and water, enthralled. Plant had indeed made a persuasive case against the legitimacy of Notre Dame's title to the land on which it stood. Plant might have received a doctorate on the basis of the research he had done on this. He should have entered his hobby horse in the race.

Leone had had only a vague conception of Badin before he read Plant's manuscript. The first priest ordained in the United States, in Baltimore, had lived a roving ministry going to Bardstown, Indiana, Michigan — before they were states, of course — buying up land out of who knew what selfless greed. His deal with Sorin was lavishly narrated and documented. How could Edward Sorin fail to fear when his title to the land was contested in the late 1850s? But it was Plant's mention of natural law that triggered something deep and obscure in Leone's memory.

The Unwritten Law had dubious status in the courts, but in the Church it was the rock on which alone positive law could be justly built. Half an hour's reading made clear that such a complaint would be laughed out of any court. But Leone had found the unexpected

45

something which would enable him to triumph once more over the university counsel. How could Notre Dame dismiss as irrelevant the natural law of which the Church claimed to be the providential custodian?

The ice melted in Leone's drink, he stopped lighting cigarettes, he closed the manuscript and stared into space. A small smile formed on his lips. Victory was in that smile.

7

Although it was only Thursday, the campus had already begun to swarm with visitors for Saturday's game with the Seminoles. Early arriving Florida State fans registered in their various local hotels and then descended on the campus wearing elements of their school's regalia. War bonnets were seen and tomahawks flourished. A mocassined man of middle age, gone in drink — thus verifying perhaps the claim that alcohol should be kept from the red man and his friends — jumped into the reflecting pool in front of Hesburgh Library. The pool was three feet deep. His feathered head did not protect him when he struck bottom. He was pulled sputtering over the surrounding ledge, spitting out water. Then he gave out a spine-tingling war whoop. It would be an exciting game.

Phil had invited guests for the game, one that drew national attention of a special kind. Even in the dullest season, every Notre Dame game made it onto national television. A losing team provided solace for the many who hated the Fighting Irish and what was thought to be their unjust hold on the country's attention. Loyal fans from coast to coast gathered around their sets, certain that the Blessed Mother would pull victory out of the hat. But this was a winning season for Notre Dame and Florida State too was unbeaten. Warring statistical accounts, put together by analysts who in another age would have studied the entrails of birds, professed to show that Notre Dame's schedule could not match that of Florida State. Defenders pointed to the scope of the Irish schedule, their opponents drawn from all the major conferences, while Florida State only dominated its own conference. As the game drew near, arguments became heated, level heads were needed to prevent partisans from coming to blows. Phil's guests, Muggs Bofield and Charlie Callahan, were aficionados of the game itself and professed to be above mere partisan judgments. But the two men were divided on the possible outcome of the game. Listening to them, Roger wondered how a point could spread. He went off to his study to ponder this Euclidean problem.

When he checked his e-mail, he found a message from Father Carmody, courtesy of the young computer whiz at Holy Cross House where Carmody resided and where "young" meant a priest in his early seventies.

"Call me. Carmody."

Call me Ishmael, Roger thought, and picked up the phone. The chiding voice of a nurse informed him it was too late to put through a call to a resident. It was nearly nine o'clock.

"Could I leave a message?"

"For Father Carmody?"

"Yes."

"What is it?"

"Call me. Roger."

"Is that all?"

"He'll understand."

Father Carmody had himself driven over to the Knights' apartment the following morning. Philip, feeling the effects of his late-night seminar on college football with his two visitors, was not a pretty sight when he went to answer the door. The undeniably clerical persona before him, a type rather than Father Carmody his particular self, made Philip even more affable than, under the circumstances, he would have been to their friend. Now he saw the priest as a trophy he might display to his guests at breakfast.

"Breakfast?" Father Carmody said, looking at his watch. The priest rose and retired early and this had a distinct advantage. "Is Roger here?"

Roger had half listened when Philip went to

49

the door, but when he recognized the voice of Father Carmody he wheeled away from his computer and faced the priest as he came into the study.

"You got my message?"

They said this in unison, then laughed, Roger more boisterously than Father Carmody. The priest took a chair with a rigid back and lowered himself into it, adjusting his spine to the welcome support of the chair. He had come with a specific request.

"I would have put it to Philip, but he seems . . ."

"He was up late. He has visitors here for the game."

"Who are we playing?"

"Florida State."

"The Seminoles," the priest murmured. "That was an Indian tribe, wasn't it."

"Yes it was."

"That's why I'm here." He readjusted his back against the chair. Father Carmody suffered from lower back pain. "Indians. The university is being sued, or is at least threatened with a suit, over the land on which it is built."

It did not surprise Roger that an elderly priest resident in the Congregation's retirement home should come to him with a request from the administration, not when that priest was Father Carmody. The old priest was not, of course, among the chancellor's confidants and advisors — he had indignantly rejected this suggestion when Roger once had made it, indeed, he seemed about to say more before years of self-control stilled him. Father Carmody was someone called in when the solution to a pressing problem eluded the usual privy council or required more than usual discretion.

Roger followed the excellent rule of not indicating that he had any prior knowledge of what Father Carmody had to say. It was always best to permit an uninterrupted narrative. Afterward, he could see how it comported with the snippets he had already picked up from Professor Otto Ranke. And of course most of what Carmody told him was new.

Bartholomew Leone, a nemesis of the university, had contacted Ballast, the university counsel, with a request that they enter into negotiations on the recent dismissal of Orion Plant from the graduate program in history. Since there seemed absolutely nothing to discuss there once Ballast consulted the history department, he assumed that the charge that academic regulations had been unjustly breached was a decoy.

"This former graduate student is the source

of the charge that Father Sorin knowingly bought stolen property, stolen from the Indians, and that therefore the land should revert to the Indians. Or their heirs."

"Is Orion Plant one of them?"

"That is the assumption. Why else would he turn some humdrum historical research into a crusade?"

"Why indeed?"

Father Carmody sat forward, then thought better of it and eased his back against the firm support of the chair.

"I think you'll agree that a good offense is the best defense."

It sounded like one of the truisms that had been spoken in high slurred voices late into the night. "Of course."

Father Carmody ticked off the episodes that had enjoyed a brief run in the local media and then drifted into that great black hole that swallows up the news. Roger had not known of the episode at the log chapel. Father Carmody waved his hand.

"That doesn't matter. It is the vandalism in the cemetery that presents an unequivocal instance of law breaking."

"But more distasteful than legally serious."

"No doubt. Then there is the kidnapping."

"Father Burnside?"

"No no. The chancellor."

This was indeed news. The events Father Carmody related had been successfully kept secret. The pathetic performance of the chancellor on the video that had been left at Corby Hall was described.

"Did *they* ask for ransom?"

"*They* want a concession that the land is stolen."

"But *they* did not keep the chancellor prisoner until they got it."

"The next message told his whereabouts and rescuers went to fetch him. It has left him shaken."

"I'm not surprised."

The theory in the Main Building was that recent events had been elements in a carefully planned strategy that would stretch into an indefinite future, with more pressure put on the university with the passage of time. Kidnapping the chancellor had been a dramatic way to get his attention. And a copy of the damning video could be delivered to a television station at any moment. It was the chancellor's particular wish that all copies of the sad scene he had enacted for his captors be destroyed.

"What offense did you have in mind?"

"They, Roger. I am a mere messenger. But in this case I think they may actually be right. The assumption they want explored is that the same people are behind the legal threat and perpetrated those outrages."

"That seems plausible."

"Proof is needed. And discretion, of course; the other side must not be alerted that the inquiry is going on."

"And you want Philip to conduct it?"

"You and Philip."

An accuser accused of sacrilege and kidnapping would be thrown from his moral high horse and lose the rhetorical advantage that agitating for Indians undoubtedly gave in the present atmosphere. Roger said he was certain Philip would agree to take the case.

"Are you going to the game, Father?"

"I prefer to watch it at Holy Cross House. We have a very large screen television now."

"Can you hear the cheers from the stadium there?"

"Some of us can."

8

Professor Ranke lived with his wife and daughter in a modest ranch house on Angela Boulevard, on the edge of the campus and within easy walking distance of his office in Decio. The interview with Orion Plant not only spelled the end of the young man's academic career but also wrote finis to another matter Ranke had driven into the deeper recesses of memory. But this disturbing thought emerged then. Orion and Laverne Ranke, his daughter. Once there had been what in an eighteenth-century novel would have been called an understanding between them. Nothing overt, simply the significance of the unstated, the logic of events. In his first years as a graduate student, Orion had been a frequent presence in the Ranke home. The first time he had been included in a group of students the professor had in for a Sunday afternoon sherry party. Laverne, a recent graduate of Saint Mary's and of the same age as these graduate students, joined the party, along with Freda, Mrs. Ranke.

Otto Ranke had carried into his private life

the high standards of his profession — or was it perhaps vice versa. In any case, he would never have been able to fly in the face of facts. Laverne was what Pascal said Cleopatra would have had to be if the course of history were to have been different. There were angles from which her nose did not seem overly large. Her eyes were good, but she wore glasses with weak lenses and frames meant to draw attention away from the protuberance that supported them. Laverne had her mother's complexion, a sort of off-white that paled throughout the fall and then became splotchy with cold weather. Laverne's one undeniable endowment was her hair, inherited from the Ranke side. Thick, reddish, undulant, it swept back from her narrow forehead and formed a great distracting compensation for her face. Ranke had sometimes thought that if Laverne could back into a room she would overwhelm. She and young Plant hit it off.

He returned with the excuse of seeing his professor, but he asked about Laverne and she was summoned. Soon the murmur of their conversation and sudden bursts of laughter came from the family room at the back of the house that overlooked Cedar Grove Cemetery. Freda and Otto looked at one another but said nothing. Those visits had become regular. Laverne would make popcorn and they would watch any silliness on television in order to remain in the family room and away from her parents in the front part of the house. They went out infrequently — as often as not to a movie shown on campus — but he was a graduate student living on a pittance. They developed the lugubrious habit of going across the backyard for long walks in Cedar Grove Cemetery.

Ranke did not deny that the apparent direction of his daughter's relations with Orion Plant affected his treatment of the young man. Like most graduate students, Orion had arrived with an inflated notion of the state of his knowledge. This was followed by a dip in the slough of despond when the extent of the ignorance they had brought with them was revealed in class and seminar. Orion skipped this second phase and thus never advanced to the third desirable condition when the demands of the discipline were understood and a chastened confidence began. Orion remained as he had come, unaware of the vast gaps in his learning. And then one day, in Ranke's office, Orion casually mentioned that he had married.

Hope leapt in the professorial breast. Laverne had gone off to visit a classmate in Detroit some days before. Had the young couple eloped? Was this his son-in-law who sat before him, simpering and foolish?

"She's from a local family. She works in the Huddle."

Otto Ranke had never confronted such a situation in his entire life. The father in him suggested bounding over his desk and throttling this callous fool. After a moment, his stolid Teutonic ancestry took over.

"Well," he said.

"It came as a bit of a surprise to me too."

Had Laverne been told of this new attachment that had led so swiftly to the altar? Ranke did not press Orion for details. He diverted the conversation to academic channels. Nothing in his manner could have conveyed to his student the contempt he felt for him. His own honor seemed to have been compromised. But all this was suppressed as they turned to the amateurish paper to which Ranke had already given a mark far higher than it deserved.

Laverne had not known. When she heard the news she languished. She became a recluse in her room. She took several days off from her job in the library and when she returned to the check-out desk she was, like so many females in library employ, one whose future was entirely behind her.

A new modus vivendi established itself between professor and student. Orion was known as his protégé and Ranke could not bring himself to make known his true estimate of the young man's prospects as an historian. He continued to dissemble with his colleagues. They came to count on him as Orion Plant's champion. Colleagues had watched with dismay his defense of the unpromising Plant, but Ranke continued to shield the young man from the judgment that should have been passed on him. And so for years it had gone.

Three months before, Ranke returned home, grunted at Freda, who tried to detain him, and went into his study. It was there that he heard emanating from the family room sounds that had seemed to be stilled forever. There was a young man with Laverne and that man was undoubtedly Orion Plante. Their conversation murmured as before, the outbursts of laughter recalled a better time. Ranke sat at his desk and did not know what to do. Later, when Orion had gone and Freda had retired with a cup of broth, Ranke confronted his daughter.

"Was that Orion I heard back here with you?"

"Yes." She looked up at him with radiant, defiant eyes.

"What was it all about?"

59

"I don't know what you mean."

"Laverne, the man is married."

"Not in the Church!"

"Not in the Church?"

"It was impulsive, but he had the good sense not to enter into a real marriage."

"Has he proposed to you?"

She wanted to say yes, he could sense that. One visit had wiped away the empty years. Things were back to status quo ante. The expectations she had, perhaps rightly, entertained before were back in full force.

"I don't want you entertaining a married man in this house."

He left her to ponder what he would have been happy to generalize into a Kantian universal. No self-respecting father would care to have his unmarried daughter murmuring and laughing with a married man in his home.

It was some time before he learned that what he had thought was a solitary visit, a nostalgic return of the faithless beau, had been the first of a renewed series. Freda colluded with the young couple, moved by the status of Orion's marriage. Not even an annulment would be needed, only a divorce as civil as the marriage.

"Then he has proposed?"

Freda seemed confused.

"So he hasn't?"

"But, Otto, he is back . . ."

Laverne was no more informative. She was openly defiant now, displaying that madness of the female in want of a mate. How powerful is the drive of nature that she could find the man who had broken her heart acceptable once more. There was something fresh and animated about her. She might have been wakened from a long sleep. Ranke repeated his order about her seeing Orion in his home, but it was no longer a Kantian imperative. Perhaps something could happen even now . . .

The clandestine meetings continued. Months passed. Orion continued living with his wife and her family. Should Otto ask him what his intentions were?

All indecision left him when the headstones in the cemetery were toppled and he learned that Laverne had been entertaining Orion while her father attended a lecture by a visitor to campus. Otto Ranke saw it all. His daughter had been cruelly used again, and the fact that she was unaware of it made it worse. She had provided a base of operations for the desecration in Cedar Grove. He was sure of it, intuitively certain. The canons of his profession did not warrant the inference, but doubt was a stranger in this matter. How easy to slip out of the house, into the cemetery, and then back again, unobserved by any campus patrol that might have been in the vicinity. A few days later, at the meeting of the graduate committee, Otto Ranke added his black ball to the others and Orion Plant was ejected. Laverne languished. There were no further visits. Professor Ranke found it difficult to rejoice in his Pyrrhic victory. His daughter, having twice taken leave of her senses, now took a leave from her post in the library. Freda was confused but silent.

Professor Ranke was seated in his study, brooding, ignoring the sounds of pre-game celebration that turned the campus into swarming crowds of anticipation, when the call from Roger Knight came.

9

Professor Ranke suggested they meet in his home. He did not go to campus on game days.

"Wait until the game has started, then come. The campus is deserted and the roads are passable."

Roger agreed. His usual mode of transportation on campus was a golf cart and, as the professor had said, it would be an easy matter to drive it from the apartment he and Philip shared in graduate student housing to the Ranke home on Angela. It was two-thirty in the afternoon when he set out. The trees were golden, falling leaves drifted in a variety of graceful spirals onto the campus lawns. From the stadium came as from a great distance the strains of band music and the low guttural sound of the eighty thousand spectators which from time to time erupted into a roar that seemed to shake more leaves from the trees. Not ten minutes after setting out, Roger rolled up the Ranke driveway and began the slow process of extricating himself from the cart. The front door opened and Ranke stood there, sweatered, slippered, smoking his pipe, waiting for Roger to approach.

"Can I help you?"

"I'll manage."

And he did. He lumbered toward his host and allowed himself to be helped up the steps and into the house. As they went on to the study, a wraithlike young woman looked at them from a doorway.

"My daughter, Laverne."

Roger bowed. The wraith withdrew.

"I have come on a curious mission," Roger said when he had been eased into a large leather chair. The walls of the room were lined with books. The surface of the desk was cluttered in an attractive way. On either side of the chair, books were scattered on the floor, some open, some shut.

"Forgive me for not meeting you on campus."

"Nonsense. I understand perfectly." A distant roar went up in the stadium where Philip and his guests were following the fortunes of the game between Notre Dame and Florida State.

"I see your property abuts the cemetery." He had noticed this as he purred along the walk that passed the three entrances to Cedar Grove.

"They will not have to carry me far."

Roger laughed, sensing this was a standard remark when the proximity of the house to Cedar Grove was mentioned.

"Little else commends this location other than the fact that I can walk to campus. But on a day like today . . ." Ranke lifted his hands and let them drop. Earlier, game traffic had whisked along Angela Boulevard to the parking lots, but now the street was quieter than at any other time. Ranke settled back in his desk chair. "Most of my colleagues fled to the northern suburbs. Their houses look out on artificial lakes and golf courses. They insist it is charming. But I would have to drive."

"And look out on artificial lakes and a golf course."

Ranke smiled. "What will you drink?"

"Nothing."

"I am going to have some beer."

"Do. I never take alcohol myself, but you must have your beer."

"Mrs. Ranke can serve you coffee."

"Perfect."

Roger had the sense that Ranke was trying to postpone whatever it was that had brought Roger here. Why did he think that Ranke already knew?

"Once you mentioned a graduate student who was working on the early days of the university."

"He has been dismissed."

"Then he is Orion Plant."

"I forgot that I mentioned his name."

"You didn't."

Roger sipped the hot strong coffee and put cup and saucer on the hassock before him. The shortest distance between two points is a straight line. He told Ranke why he had come.

"So they suspect Orion."

"You don't seem surprised."

"What reason do they have?"

"It is largely inference. He has retained a lawyer to contest his dismissal from the graduate school."

"Good God."

"He has no case?"

"The department should be sued for pretending he had the capacity to be a historian. I should be. As his advisor I gave him the benefit of every doubt. Finally that became impossible."

"You agreed to his dismissal?"

"I voted for it."

"Do you think it possible that he was responsible for what was done in Cedar Grove?"

"Oh yes. But why such concern about actions which, however ignoble, would not be worth prosecuting?"

"There are other things."

Ranke squirmed in his chair when Roger told him of the arrested wedding at the log chapel, but of course he had heard of that. But the kidnapping of the chancellor astonished him.

"That is being kept absolutely confidential, of course."

"Of course. Let me see if I understand you."

Ranke had a gift for succinctness. But when the story was made short it had its unsavory aspect. The university intended to gather evidence, if there was any, that Plant had been behind these events. The kidnapping loomed largest. Then, rather than have Plant prosecuted they intended to use this information to undermine any suit Plant proposed to bring against the university.

"That's the idea," Roger agreed.

"This seems very large artillery to destroy an insect."

"Remember, I never met the man."

"It was only an analogy. Surely there are simpler ways to handle a man who threatens to bring a suit with absolutely no merit against the university."

"There is a larger target."

Ranke lifted his unbarbered brows and finished his glass of beer. His pipe had gone out and he began relighting it. He was waiting.

"What had Plant discovered about the transfer of the land to Notre Dame?"

"I don't know."

"I had hoped he had shown you his research as it was done. Isn't that the usual procedure with a doctoral dissertation?"

"He had long wandered away from the topic we had approved. He was an erratic student, subject to obsessions. The plight of the Indians, the alleged plight, became everything to him."

"Did you talk to him about it?"

"I pressed him for chapters of the dissertation he was supposedly writing."

Roger had the feeling that Ranke could tell him more but would not. He had come in the hope that Ranke would prove a short cut to whatever might constitute the basis for an accusation that the university counsel was sure would be made, to the vast embarrassment of Notre Dame. Roger had no compunction in helping stave off that embarrassment. He had no doubt that Native Americans had been badly treated here, though he did not think this could be laid at Father Sorin's door. In any case, attempts to reverse all the injustices of the past would make a shambles of the world as it had come to be. On the continent, in the Middle East, in Ireland, such disputes led to armed conflict that created fresh injustices for future generations to ponder.

"I love your book on famous authors who lectured at Notre Dame."

Authorial vanity, fully justified in Otto Ranke's case, altered the atmosphere in the study. His host called for more beer and coffee, which was brought by the broad and beaming *hausfrau* who was Mrs. Ranke. For two hours they sat happily recalling a golden past. When Roger rose — with Ranke's help — to return to his apartment before the game ended, they passed once more through the living room to the front door. And, as before, the spectral Laverne looked accusingly at them as they passed her.

10

The incident at halftime was within the sight of all eighty thousand spectators in the stadium, but only a fraction took notice. While the Florida State band played there would of course be flag twirlers and other supernumeraries clothed in the somewhat romantic costumes in which the natives of the hemisphere were thought to have dressed, but no such garb was expected when the Notre Dame band, the oldest college band in the nation, as the announcer said in reverberating tones and, one hoped, with historical justification, took the field. Throughout the game the Leprechaun had pranced about dressed like a stage Irishman, wearing a cottony false beard, taking part with the cheerleaders. But the character that took the field as one band marched off and the other prepared to occupy the gridiron was a sight never before seen in that hallowed place.

He might have been mistaken for the Leprechaun had it not been for the feathered headdress he wore. Onto the field he came, his body bowed back in what might have been mimicry of the bandleader, head so far back that his feathers seemed to brush against the grass of the field. In a moment it became clear that his was an unscheduled appearance. A hand went up to halt the band about to take the field. The feathered apparition advanced to the fifty yard line before coming to a halt. There, he bowed first to one side of the field, and then the other. There was a murmur of tentative laughter and those descending to the lower level for refreshments slowed their pace.

Suddenly, with one deft movement, the figure divested himself of his green costume and was exposed in near nakedness, wearing only a breech cloth. His upper body was luridly painted and he spread his arms wide. Then, with obvious dexterity he began to unfurl the banner that had been wrapped around his ostensible baton. The wind caught the cloth as it was freed and then the banner floated free, its legend legible to those on the Notre Dame side. GIVE NOTRE DAME BACK TO THE INDIANS.

The reaction was equivocal until the uniformed security men who had been gathering on the sidelines converged on him. Some minutes were taken up in a comic pursuit, as again and again he eluded the hands that would take him captive. The crowd re-

71

sponded to an evident underdog and began to cheer his many escapes, but then he was subdued and taken in custody from the field. Boos were heard, and jeers directed at the captors rather than the captive. One florid-faced guard hastily wound up the offending banner. It was all over in a matter of minutes, but the scene had gone out over television to the ends of the nation.

In the chancellor's box, consternation reigned. Father Bloom, reminded of his recent ordeal, had gone pale and replied incoherently to the queries of his distinguished guests. Someone opined that it was a student prank and was surprised at the wild and angry glare he got from the chancellor. One of the chancellor's handlers was heard to give orders that the culprit be detained.

"What was that all about?" the wife of a trustee asked.

"A student prank," the chancellor managed to say, but he said it between gritted teeth.

On the field, a planned program was executed by the band, but there was little appreciation in the box reserved for the officers of the university and their guests. It occurred to one of the proliferating platoon of assistant provosts that Noonan, chairman of the board of trustees, had been called from the box just before the first half ended. He had not yet returned. Nor had he returned when the halftime festivities were over and the opposing teams went to their respective sidelines to the cheers of their supporters.

"Who was it came for Noonan?" the chancellor asked the priest for whom the title Advisor to the Chancellor had been invented.

"An usher?" But there was doubt in the advisor's voice.

"Go find him."

He did not mean the usher. The advisor left, fighting against the flow of fans returning to their seats for the second half.

The third quarter ended and neither Noonan nor the advisor had returned to the box. The chancellor was clearly agitated. From the nearby presidential box, the university counsel came in response to an urgent gesture.

"Neither Noonan nor Father Anselm have come back."

"I'll find them."

"Take an escort with you."

The thought that anyone who left would fail to return had the chancellor in its grip. Ballast nodded grimly.

It was a glorious victory for the home team, but there was no rejoicing in the chancellor's party. Mrs. Noonan was, in her own words, frantic. Her husband had had open heart surgery within the month and, having seen him so reduced, his hitherto solid thereness brought into doubt by the surgery, the valedictory thoughts she'd had while he was being operated on returned. The chancellor was in no condition to reassure her. Ballast's failure to come back with word filled him with foreboding.

When the chancellor and his party left the box, they moved swiftly to the lower level and there, in a room reserved for security forces, the officers of the university confronted the halftime Indian. He sat in the brightly lighted room on a stool, a blanket draped around his shoulders. The paint on his body had been smeared in the struggle to take him into custody. He looked with manic cheerfulness at the administrative party. Ballast had been questioning him without result.

"He won't say who he is."

"Has he no identification?"

"Where would he carry it?"

Mrs. Noonan had begun to weep. Something was very wrong and she did not know what it was, only that her husband had missed half the game and nobody knew where he was. Miss Trafficant tried unsuccessfully to console her.

"Where is Mr. Noonan?" the chancellor demanded of the captured Indian.

"Would that be High Noonan?"

It is a serious offense against Canon Law to strike a priest; the traffic in the opposite direction is murkier. It was all the chancellor could do not to slap the smirking face of the captive. Once the highest officers of this institution would have been able to recognize any student, but neither the chancellor nor anyone in his party knew who this lad was. Of course, none of them came into regular contact with students.

"What should we do with him?" a security person asked Ballast, switching her ponytail as she did.

"Is he under arrest?"

"We don't have the authority to arrest anyone, not properly."

And so, perforce, the South Bend police were called and the cat was, or soon would be, out of the bag. The chancellor took his party to the Morris Inn, the campus hotel, in awaiting limousines. He wished he were going to his room and to his bed where he could pull the covers over his head and curse the day he had been plucked from the ranks to his present eminence. At the Morris Inn they found both Noonan and Father Anselm. Some time before, they had been pushed into the lobby,

75

cloth sacks tied over their heads, hands bound behind them, stripped to the waist. Their bodies had been painted, with especial attention paid to the scar left by Noonan's open heart surgery.

11

Orion Plant had spent the day of the football game in company with his wife, Marcia, and a graduate student in mathematics named Byers. Neither of them knew that he was establishing his alibi. He himself had had no direct contact with the man named Hessian, a mercenary in any case who was exhibitionist enough to accept the role assigned him. He thought it was a spoof, and any small reluctance he might have felt was swept away by the mention of national television. Byers had no knowledge of that particular event. Laverne had assumed the job of recruiting Hessian with dedicated loyalty and she, he was sure, would be quiet as the grave even under torture. He still had not told Marcia that he was no longer a graduate student and that now they must survive on her salary from the Huddle.

Disappointment at his dismissal had long since given way to satisfaction, as if he had deliberately arranged his own departure. He felt free. He was no longer in thrall to the pedantic demands of academic research. He had not wasted much time on his approved project, not since he had stumbled upon what Leone had called his crusade. What Orion referred to, not facetiously, as the Younger archives had set him on the path that would take him on to glory. Whatever the outcome of his efforts, the name Orion Plant was assured of a permanent place in the annals of Notre Dame.

The bedroom that had been occupied by Mrs. Younger before she took refuge with a married son in San Diego had been converted into a war room of research. A plain table sat among the cabinets holding the records of Younger Real Estate, but Orion's attention had been concentrated on papers that dated from the nineteenth century. There he had come upon the plat book of property the Youngers had owned on land now occupied by the new golf course. There had been a house, of course, but it was only the ownership of the land that was of interest in the plat book. The name Andrew Jackson had caught his attention, and then Chief Pokagon's. To Orion's cold eye it was clear that Marcia's forbears had jobbed the Indians out of that land at least at several removes. Under the aegis of Andrew Jackson it had passed from the Indians to white ownership and then in a direct line to Silas Younger, Marcia's great-great-grandfather. From that point on, work on his dissertation had become a distraction and he had pursued the spoor from cabinet drawer to cabinet drawer.

"Your relatives were natural historians," he told Marcia. She smiled as if unsure this was a compliment. But in the Younger operation no piece of paper was considered too unimportant to be filed away and kept.

The dossier Orion had given to Leone the lawyer was but a sampling of the goods he had gotten on the university. At the beginning, he had been motivated by a generic iconoclasm. Notre Dame was a volatile mixture of braggadocio and inferiority complex. The fact that he had been accepted by no other graduate program was held against him when he arrived, as if, he grumbled, he had aimed at the bottom and hit it.

"I didn't apply anywhere else."

"That wasn't wise. You were lucky to get in here."

This vacillation between self-deprecation and chest-thumping bravura fascinated for a time. It was difficult to tell which was genuine and which bogus. How could an institution draw constant attention to its rankings by one magazine or another and at the same time insist on its uniqueness? To be in the top twenty-five was perhaps comparable to being number one, but aside from football and philosophy that ranking had eluded Notre Dame. With time he became disgusted with this constant looking in the mirror for reassurance. True self-confidence would have dictated indifference to the vagaries of magazine staffs who presumed to assess the colleges and universities of the nation. Yet the current ranking was prominently featured on the university website.

It is, of course, of the nature of graduate students to grumble and when in private assembly to damn the program and mock the faculty. But this, too, was ambiguous, a hedge against possible failure. With Orion it became wholly sincere. His contempt for his discipline was not localized. He came to despise the pointless pedantic dissertations his peers were engaged in writing. What earthly difference would one outcome or another of their research make? Professor Ranke might regard his delving into the past of the place as a diversion, but it had become a holy war for Orion. Marcia was his ally, but only up to a point. Laverne, whom she scornfully called the "professor's daughter," was a sore point.

"She's a double agent, O."

007? He tried to josh away her suspicions. But he had grievances of his own. At her insistence, he had included Byers in the tribal councils, as he called them.

"He's in mathematics."

"Even so."

It was as if she wanted to balance his inclusion of Laverne. To tell Marcia that admitting Laverne to the campaign was a way of compromising Ranke would have been met with derision. But Orion really didn't trust Byers. Byers had been there at the log chapel when they disrupted the wedding in the name of the wronged Indians, but he pleaded an examination when it was a question of kidnapping the chancellor. Byers might have been making sure that he was minimally involved and keeping out of harm's way. And Orion had the sense that he had never forgotten that once Marcia had been his girl.

But Byers was there when they ringed the television set to see the fake leprechaun prance onto the field and then tear off his green disguise to reveal his painted body. They cheered as he escaped again and again from the clutches of the security forces.

"He certainly earned his money."

Fifty dollars, collected from the reluctant group of conspirators. Orion had tossed in a twenty to sweeten the pot, avoiding Marcia's eyes.

Later, someone commended Laverne on

her choice and Marcia bristled. "He'll be arrested, you know. He'll tell them everything. Let's see what Laverne does then."

Orion stood and put on his coat. Marcia looked up. "Where are you going?"

"I'm going to check out the Morris Inn, see how they're taking it."

He did not see Marcia look at Byers.

12

The Morris Inn was packed after the game. Fans of the opposing teams had forgotten the animosities that preceded the contest and were now toasting one another in a show of good sportsmanship. The chancellor was not there, having been whisked away to a more controllable post-game celebration on the fourteenth floor of the library, an aerie from which the now emptied stadium was visible to the south, the campus to the west, Mishawaka, its mall and many satellites to the east, and to the north the long lines of traffic heading for the toll road.

The chancellor was drinking Evian on ice with a twist. His party were imbibing more enervating potions before they went in to dinner hosted by the president. The hours all this would consume lay before the chancellor like a penitential task. He was finding it difficult to keep his chin up and show the flag in the customary way. These happy people were directly or indirectly responsible for the affluence of the university and this was small compensation for their loyal labor. Behind the chancellor's smile, hidden from those with whom he exchanged banalities, was the memory of that half-dressed madman streaking up and down the field carrying his banner. It was one more move in a game he understood only as an effort to torment him. Suddenly, tall cadaverous Sisson stood before him, tipping his head forward so that he could both look down at the chancellor and look over his glasses.

"Another triumph." Sisson's voice was heavy with sarcasm. He represented the persistent effort of some alumni to have football de-emphasized, to stop what they thought was a drift toward secularization. Sisson wanted all theologians to take the oath prescribed by Canon Law for teachers of Catholic doctrine. He wanted the chancellor to initiate and lead a movement on the part of other chancellors to accept *Ex corde ecclesiae*, the document on Catholic universities, unreservedly. Sisson scoffed at the excuse of academic freedom. He laughed at the suggestion that a more militantly Catholic Notre Dame would have difficulty raising money. He claimed that he himself could raise more but too many potential donors were put off by the direction the university was taking. Sisson himself possessed unmeasured wealth and he was generous to a fault, the fault being that he carefully earmarked the money he gave for projects of which he approved. Now he began a litany of complaints, things that had been passed on to him by students and faculty. Father Bloom felt under seige and abandoned by the president and his minions. He almost welcomed the bustling arrival of Ballast.

"Mr. Sisson," the university counselor cried. Sisson leaned forward to look at Ballast. He seemed not to remember him. "I'm going to have to ask Father to come aside with me for a moment."

Sisson dismissed them. Ballast got a good grip on the chancellor's arm and led him away to the area by the elevators.

"He's been arrested."

"Is he a student?"

"He says not."

"Then who is he?"

"He says his name is Tonto."

"He's part of it."

He did not need to explain to the counsel what the whole was. Ballast had entered eagerly into the chancellor's theory that there was a vendetta against him.

"As chancellor," Ballast insisted.

"I'm beginning to think it's me they're after."

"The immediate question is, do we ask that charges be pressed or dismiss it as a harmless joke?"

"Harmless! He was on national television."

"His message will be seen as a joke."

"But is it?" There was desperation in the chancellor's eyes.

"Half the staff of the archives is working on it." Ballast got on tiptoe to whisper into Father Bloom's ear. "And the Knight brothers."

"Ah." He sipped his Evian as if from need. Afterward he worked his lips like a woman who had just applied lipstick. "Have him prosecuted."

"You're sure."

"Absolutely. We have to strike back." He paused. "Check with the president, of course."

Leif Quinlan, as his name suggested, was a hybrid. On the paternal side, he was disposed to be loyal to the university where he had taught some twenty-five years; on the maternal side he was a Viking eager to descend on the coast of Ireland and strike fear in the hearts of the inhabitants. Quinlan was president of the faculty senate and member ex officio of all its standing committees. Under his direction, the senate had perfected its techniques of harassing the administration, invoking the stated mission of the university against its actual practices. Quinlan had not shown his reluctance when he gave the green light to the campaign against the administration's cruel treatment of homosexuals. Homosexuals already controlled, through puppets, the student publications and were the constant object of friendly attention there. But their organization was not officially recognized by the university so they had to add to their numbers in the usual way. Quinlan was personally appalled by the salacious solicitations written minutely between the tiles over urinals; he had stopped looking at the graffiti vandalously inscribed on desktops in the classrooms. Quinlan had once been a Marine and had been taught harsh ways of dealing with the phenomenon. But now he was a professor and a senator, and principle was principle. Academic freedom was at stake. The Inquisition must be held at bay. When the chancellor made his biannual appearance before the senate — a custom and not a requirement — Quinlan badgered him mercilessly on the subject. But his heart of hearts was not in it. The recent calling into question of the legitimacy of the university's possession of the land on which it stood had come as a blessed relief. Here was an issue to which he could devote less troubled enthusiasm.

"Was he a student?" Trepani the sociologist asked without preamble. Her chipmunk teeth did not need her wicked smile to be seen.

"What else?"

"I hope they persecute him."

But this course required a straightforward spunk that had not seemed in great supply in the administration. He feared that they would seek to wriggle free of a definite stand.

"We must pray that they will."

"I will speak to Anita Trafficant." There was a sisterhood of solidarity among the females on campus which encompassed faculty and staff and even one or two gate guards.

"Do that."

Trepani closed her mouth and seemed to be biting her lower lip. She nodded resolutely and went away.

Quinlan had confidence in her. Meanwhile, he moved among the fans in the lobby of the Morris Inn as a Greek god might have moved among the foe of the forces he favored. No one recognized him here and he felt the enormous power of anonymity. These were the rabid fans, the big donors, the plutocrats for whom the university could do no wrong. He was delighted to hear references to the halftime interruption. Some laughed, others frowned. In either case, the deed had registered. Quinlan was determined that the senate would stand behind that plucky lad. He would call an emergency meeting of the inner council of the senate on the morrow. His arm was jostled and he turned to face an irked expression.

"Sorry."

"Where's the chancellor?" Something in this fellow's proletarian scowl caused Quinlan to make a leap of logic. Could this be one of them? "Oh, they're in the library, probably discussing how to handle the lad who spoiled halftime for them."

"What will they do?"

"Have him prosecuted, I suppose."

The scowl gave way to a smile. "Do you think so?"

"Do you know who I am?"

"No."

"President of the faculty senate. Leif Quinlan."

The small eyes focused and seemed to recognize a friend.

"Are you one of them?" Leif asked.

"Why do you ask?"

"The senate intends to back him all the way."

"Good!"

"What's your name?"

"It doesn't matter."

"It does to me."

Pros and cons took serial possession of the little eyes. "Plant."

"Just Plant?"

"Orion."

Quinlan put out his hand and, after hesitating, Orion Plant took it. Thus their solidarity was expressed.

13

On Monday, before seeking out Professor Ranke's now former graduate student, Roger Knight stopped by the university archives to consult with Greg Whelan. The archivist was at work in his cubbyhole and Roger paused in the door, not wanting to disturb his friend. They had not spoken for some time and he realized how he missed their conversations. Whelan was replete with lore about the university and he knew the archives like the back of his hand. Once he might have lamented the fact that his stammer had closed off the avenues his doctorate and his later law degree qualified him to travel, but his handicap had stood athwart both paths and he had resigned himself to becoming a librarian. This had landed him in the archives and from the first day there he felt he had come home.

He turned, startled, then smiled. "Roger." It was a blessing of their friendship that Whelan did not stammer when they talked, his handicap neutralized by Roger's obesity.

"You're busy."

Whelan rose from his computer as if to indicate the relative unimportance of his task. They moved to one of the closed rooms where visiting scholars worked but which this morning was empty so they could converse without danger of disturbing some important research.

"Recent events have made me curious about the university's title to its land."

Whelan smiled. *"Moi aussi.* I have been creating a list of relevant items."

"I should like to see it."

"I'll print it out for you."

"Any surprises?"

The archives were a treasure house of surprises and even Whelan, with his encyclopedic grasp of their contents, was constantly coming upon the unexpected. He had no need of his recent assembled list of items to recall what he had found. Roger listened enthralled. He was no longer surprised by Whelan's memory: it would have rivaled that of a medieval master who had to hold in store hundreds of texts seen once and then no more.

Father Badin's 1832 purchase of the land from the government was well documented and had been told in all the standard works. He had spent only a few years at the mission he established there, building the log chapel and several sheds, and ministering to the

Potowatomi. In 1835, he was off again, after deeding the land to the diocese of Vincennes. Father Petit was one of the priests who succeeded him at Ste.-Marie-des-Lacs, as Badin called the mission. This was the property offered to Edward Sorin by the bishop of Vincennes. A few years later, Badin took up residence at what was now the University of Notre Dame, receiving an annuity from Father Sorin, a species of retirement plan that would make his many years lie less heavily on his shoulders. But there had been misunderstanding almost from the beginning. Badin was a shrewd bargainer but he had more than met his match in Sorin. Whelan gave a swift precis of this oft-told story and then stopped. His expression was promissory.

"What then?"

"Attention is then drawn to legitimacy of the transfer to Sorin of title to the land."

"Ah."

This story was unknown to Roger and he listened attentively. Whelan looped back to the saga of Father Petit, who had identified himself with the dispossessed natives and when they were herded away had gone with them, as friend, as chaplain, as fellow martyr. He was buried in the crypt of Sacred Heart.

"I have developed a devotion to him," Whelan confided. "I often visit him there."

This straightforward acceptance of the communion of the saints warmed Roger's heart. How few moved from acceptance of the doctrine to its realization. Saints have written of the angels that attend the altar on which the Mass is offered, the Church Triumphant as well as the Church Suffering there with the Church Militant as the central event in cosmic history was commemorated. For Whelan, Petit was a contemporary, separated only by the veil of death.

"But that was before Sorin came?"

"And after Badin."

"Ah."

Whelan went on. Speaking as a lawyer, he doubted that either Badin's or Sorin's title to the land could successfully be contested.

"Besides, who has status to contest it?"

"Descendants?"

"You must read of the death march to the Southwest to see how improbable that is."

"Could someone come forward on behalf of those Indians?"

"They could try."

"I think they are."

Although cleared of snow, the campus walks were icy and Roger made slow progress in his golf cart to Juniper Road across which he inched, hoping he was sufficiently visible

94

to traffic. Motorists sometimes seemed to think that if they had a clear shot at a crossing student they could take him out with impunity. He reached the library parking lot and headed across it as if it were frozen tundra. The tire treads were packed with snow and had lost their traction. An icy wind whipped at him, changing directions constantly as if to assault him on all sides. When he reached Bulla Road, he headed east toward the house where Orion Plant lived.

Once this road had been lined with residences. Now the Day Care Center and the vast village containing the buildings which housed graduate students commanded it. In one of those buildings was the apartment Roger shared with Philip, and he felt a powerful impulse to postpone his mission and return to the warmth of his workroom and his computer. But talking with Whelan had made this visit seem even more important. What he and Phil had been commissioned to do was something he could do more easily than his brother. Faculty status should be an Open Sesame to the Plant residence.

Five minutes spent shivering on the doorstep, wondering if he should sound the bell yet again, made Roger doubt he would be admitted. Lights were on, he had the sense that someone was in the house, though the racket of the wind would have whisked away any sound that might have come to him, even if his ears had not been hidden away beneath the woolen cap he had pulled down firmly over his head. There was a taste of winter in the air, though the prediction was that there were still warm weeks ahead. Indian Summer.

Finally there was the sound of the door being unlocked. It was opened and someone was vaguely visible through the steamed glass of the door. A woman's hand cleared a porthole and peered out. Roger pulled off his hat and shouted to the wind that he was Professor Knight. Finally the storm door was unlocked and pushed open. Roger heaved himself inside and fell onto the sofa, huffing and puffing.

"Thank you. Is your husband home?"

"Who are you?"

"Roger Knight. Professor Knight."

"In history?" Her manner had changed from wary to sympathetic when he sat on the sofa without hesitation. Now she was wary again.

"No, no. I am a university professor." He smiled. "A man without a country."

She was an unprepossessing young woman. Suddenly a man appeared from another room. He stood and looked with disappointment at Roger.

"I've heard of you."

"Word gets around. I know your dissertation director Otto Ranke rather well. He mentioned you."

Orion's reaction to this was edgy and odd. He swung on his wife. "Get us some coffee, why don't you?"

She gave an impatient sigh and then said to Roger, "Would you like coffee?"

"Please. Not for me."

"I want coffee," the presumed Orion said, glaring at her.

"Then I'll have some too," Roger said cheerfully. He had a hunch that Orion had not told his wife of the demise of his academic life. This seemed an advantage of some sort, he wasn't sure why.

"So you know Ranke?" his host said when they were alone.

"I'm Roger Knight." Roger rocked forward and extended his hand.

"Orion Plant." They shook hands. "So you know old Ranke?"

"I was reminded of something he once told me about things that have been happening on campus."

"What things?"

"Silly things, by and large. I didn't see it myself, but I understand someone dressed as an Indian brave made himself conspicuous during halftime."

"I heard about that."

"You weren't at the game?"

"I never go." Roger had met members of that fraction of Notre Dame people who professed never to follow any university sport, never to have seen a game. But it was not on principle with Orion. "How's a graduate student supposed to afford a ticket?"

"I suppose the stipend is small."

Orion looked thoughtfully at him. "What exactly did Professor Ranke say about me that brought you out on a day like this?"

"It is terrible weather. Totally different from Saturday. I don't suppose any one would run around half clothed on a day like today."

"You seem fascinated by that."

"Actually, it was merely a catalyst. Not unlike the wedding at the log chapel a few weeks ago."

"What was that?"

"You don't know?"

He might just as well have denied hearing of the halftime incident. If anything, the disrupted, or at least postponed, wedding, received more attention. Certainly student attention. Perhaps they imagined their own future weddings made a pawn of by someone's idea of fun. Roger described the scene, tendentiously.

"Dressing up and demonstrating is one thing, depriving someone forcibly of their freedom quite another. I say nothing of the sacrilege."

"But think of the point of it! They were protesting what was done to the Native Americans who occupied this land long before any white man came."

"Professor Ranke told me you had become quite knowledgeable about all that."

"It's a kind of hobby, only tangential to my dissertation."

"Then you think the demonstrators have a case?"

"I was there, man. I was one of them."

"The leader?"

"They wouldn't have known the facts if I hadn't told them. How could anyone know the facts and not want to do something about it?"

Mrs. Plant came in and Roger was introduced formally. She brought the coffee in mugs, black, and, having sat, asked, "Do you take anything with it?"

"This is fine."

"We always drink it black."

"Coffee. One of the white man's contributions to the continent."

"And tobacco is the Indian's gift." Orion pulled out some cigarettes and lit one defiantly. Marcia got hold of the package before he put it back in his pocket, took one, and waited for him to light it. Finally she lit it herself.

"In this case, the Indian giver is being asked to take it back."

"I've quit," Orion said. "I know I can. But I choose to smoke."

"He did quit," Marcia said in awed tones. "I never could."

"We've been talking about incidents on behalf of Indians that have taken place on campus lately," Roger said.

"Never heard of them."

Orion looked at her. "Of course you did."

"I did not."

"Are you a student, too?" Roger asked.

"I work on campus."

When Orion did speak of the way the university had acquired its land, it was a hopelessly garbled version. Perhaps deliberately so. After his visit to Whelan, Roger would scarcely have given Orion a passing mark on his presentation.

The battery in his cart was low and Roger regretted not recharging it while he talked with the Plants. He would risk that he had enough power to get home. It was only several hundred yards away. He told the Plants that as he squeezed behind the wheel.

"They stole all this land too." Orion said. Marcia, not dressed for it, had come outside too, and she clung to her husband's arm. As he drove away Roger was saddened by the thought that he had learned enough to give credence to the view that Orion had toppled gravestones and, more grave, kidnapped the chancellor, the trustee Noonan, and Father Anselm. Even so, the information was wanted to neutralize his charges, not to have him put in prison. There was consolation in that.

The wind had gone down during the interval of his visit and he got within walking distance of the apartment before the battery of his golf cart went dead.

14

Professor Otto Ranke sat in committee, his mind wandering, thinking of a recent headline in the *Observer*: GROUP DEBATES NAME OF COMMITTE. He had come to relish these proofs of student illiteracy. It was all he could do not to read the student paper with a correcting pencil. *Committee* was a word no member of the faculty was likely to misspell. How much of their time was spent, scattered around a table like this, discussing some interminable topic. This was a meeting of the college ethics committee and he was departmental representative involuntarily, having been appointed by Sencil after the chair had explained to him the refusal of junior members to do anything beyond the minimal for their exorbitant pay.

"But committee work is part of the minimum."

"I wish I could convince them of it."

"Let me try."

"No, Otto, no." The thought alarmed Sencil. He was in his forties and perhaps had some residual memory of a time when faculty taught twice as much as they did now and accepted academic tasks without complaint. Sencil's cowardice meant that the senior member of the department was expected to carry water for his delinquent juniors. Of course he accepted. The habits of a lifetime were hard to break. He had lived to regret his acquiescence.

Once, a student caught cheating was expelled without ceremony or hesitation. He had broken the sacred covenant that must obtain between teacher and student. Now, a professor brought his suspicions to this committee and they considered the case and acted as jury. They were not a hanging jury. The accused student routinely threatened to employ a lawyer. The level of proof had been raised to a point where it was virtually impossible to reach a guilty verdict. The criteria were no longer those of the academy, but of civil law. Still, complaints were brought and the committee sat.

The room they met in was a windowed seminar room off the main corridor of DeBartolo. Passersby slowed and stared at them, puzzled, and then went on. Clearly this wasn't a class and the members were so heterogenous, departmentally speaking, that their raison d'être was not obvious. An assistant dean was in the chair, a misanthrope who ignored male members and allowed sisters of her sex to preach endlessly. It didn't matter. Futility engaged in by either gender was still futility. Ranke thought of his own suspicions of only a year ago, the Russell Bacon case. It was odd to think that it had been brought to his attention by Orion Plant. Now Orion had been cast into outer darkness, rightly, while Bacon sizzled along toward his doctorate. The young man was a charlatan and a cheat.

The paper he had submitted to Ranke's seminar on the tragic history of the Congregation of Holy Cross in New Orleans that had nearly led to a break between Notre Dame and the mother house in LeMans had been passable and not much else. It happened to be on the top of the pile when Orion had come for one of his infrequent consultations. The phone rang as they were talking and Ranke answered it. A bored Plant had picked up the paper and read it. He was still holding it when Ranke finished the call.

"Why are you keeping this?"

"Those papers are from my current seminar."

"But this is my paper!"

Ranke dismissed this, saying all papers looked the same nowadays. Meaning bad. But Orion was incensed. He rattled on. He sounded like one of the cases brought before the ethics committee. But Orion was adamant. He knew his own paper, didn't he? And of course Bacon had had opportunity to download it from Orion's computer. Orion found his library carrel claustrophic and left the door open when he was in it, and unlocked when he was not.

"I keep everything on the hard disk. We talked about this assignment. I called up my old paper and gave him advice about his."

"No wonder they're similar."

"Similar? They're identical."

Orion was on his feet. He would prove it. Off he went and within the hour, he was back. He dropped a laser-printed essay on Ranke's desk.

"I'll compare them for you."

And he did, standing beside Ranke's chair, pointing back and forth between the two papers. They were line-for-line identical. Bacon had not even reformatted it before printing it out. He had remembered to substitute his name for Orion's and change the dates. In that, at least, his paper was original.

"I'm going to break his neck," Orion roared. His indignation was that of someone seldom in the right.

"Orion, sit down and listen."

Ranke explained to his presumed protégé about the ethics committee. He felt like a bad angel, corrupting the young. He was conscious of betraying, by proposed inaction, the ideals of scholarship, to say nothing of simple human honesty. Orion listened in sulking disillusionment. Ranke was patient and lengthy in his explanation of the futility of bringing any charge. When eventually Orion left, Ranke felt unclean. For once Orion had been wholly right. Bacon should have been expelled forthwith on the basis of this unequivocal evidence. In a better time, he would have been. But times had changed. Not for the first time, Otto Ranke wondered if he had not lived too long, or at least put off retirement too long.

That was not quite the end of it. Some days later, a scowling Orion returned.

"I should have stored it on a floppy," he said when he had sunk into a chair.

"What happened?"

"I told Bacon I knew what he had done."

"And he denied it."

"No. He crowed about it. Maybe if he hadn't I would just have followed your advice. I told him you knew of the plagiarism. That was my big mistake."

When Orion next looked at the files on his hard drive he found that the seminar paper was no longer there. It had been erased. It seemed clear that Bacon had done it. Any charge now would be only hearsay. Ranke felt relief and hated himself for it.

Now Ranke permitted the discussion of the ethics committee to become audible. Academic women continue to be guided by compassion, however misguided. The accused was always in good hands with them. They too had known unjust oppression. . . . Ranke took his mind out of gear again and looked out the window, not the ones giving a view of the corridor outside, but those through which the campus in the final phase of autumn was richly visible. How many more campus seasons would he see? The longer he stayed, the greater the risk that he would have someone like Bacon for a colleague. Perhaps he already did.

15

Bartholomew Leone, like everyone else, bore the effects of Original Sin. He sensed a signal victory in the offing and he was fidgety with delight. He moved up and down his office, waiting for his client, anticipating the inevitable jousting with Ballast. He had pored over the bound document Orion Plant had left with him. He had pursued the spoor of possible precedents and come up empty. Of course, academic law was relatively new and precedents were as often set as followed, but the conviction had grown upon him that Ballast would make mincemeat of him in court, if the case ever went to court, which he doubted. This was a moment when a wise lawyer threw in the sponge, advised his client he did not have a case, putting an end to it. But Leone awaited his client with a different purpose in mind.

He had not had to read much of what Orion had amassed to see its many weaknesses as the basis for a suit. But early on he had considered making the unfamiliar transition from the legal to the moral. In the time since, the idea had grown in him until he had become a veritable Torquemada in the wings. The material he had would be devastating if made public in a proper way.

To his credit it must be said that when Leone thought of his enemy it was Ballast he saw, not anyone in the administration, not any of the good fathers, at least those among the living. In some degree, it was the triumph of a higher justice that he hungered and thirsted for. But that left room for the imagined pleasure of Ballast helpless before his righteous onslaught and exposed once and for all to his employers as incompetent. But not immaterial. Ballast had taken on weight in office. Leone had it on good authority that Ballast took a slimming swim in one of the university's Olympic pools twice a week. Floated, was more probable. Well, he was soon to sink.

Something of Leone's elation dissipated when Orion Plant arrived. What a sullen, disagreeable fellow he was.

"You going to take the case?"

"Please sit down. Orion, this is more than a case."

"How do you mean?"

"I mean that we are going to take the high ground. I have sketched out a plan for a moral assault. This is too big for mere legality."

109

"I want to sue the bastards."

"That would be inadvisable."

"Have you read what I gave you?"

"Assiduously. It doesn't hold up legally. In a narrowly legal sense the land is theirs. I am willing to stipulate that. But there is a higher tribunal than the state. I needn't tell you how public opinion has swung in favor of the oppressed. Indians are regularly used in television commercials designed to wrench the heart. We will invoke the university's own high proclaimed standards against it."

"With what result?"

Leone paused. He doubted that his own triumph over Ballast would engage the sympathy of his client. It was important to proceed with care.

"How would you like being known as the man who brought Christianity to Christendom, who shook the university loose from the clutches of hypocrisy and forced it to acknowledge that you were right as rain and they despicable?"

"Will there be a settlement?"

"You mean money?"

"Of course I mean money. I am broke and without prospects. Do you realize that I have been kicked out of the university?"

"You have?" This was news indeed, but was it good or bad? "Tell me about it."

Orion spoke with the familiar whine of the disappointed academic. He lacked even the elementary skill of avoiding mention of the rules that eminently justified his ejection from graduate school. But Leone considered that the timing of Orion's separation from the university could not be better. Any fair-minded person, suitably tutored, would see that this was a transparent attempt to get rid of a whistle blower.

"Orion, you have ignited the student body. Copycat demonstrations will abound. Look at what happened at halftime."

"But no settlement."

Leone was disappointed. He had thought his own altruism would be contagious. He came down to Orion's pragmatic level.

"I think we can be assured of being well compensated for our pains. I mean the pains we inflict on the university."

Plant frowned at the universe.

"Are we agreed?"

A long, calculating moment passed. "I guess so."

"Good." Leone came around the desk and pumped his client's hand. "Just leave everything to me."

"No. I want to know everything you do before you do it."

"Of course."

As he led Orion to the door, Leone thought of ways he could disencumber himself of this disagreeable monitor. This campaign had already transcended the grudges of Orion Plant.

16

Anita Trafficant had the private secretary's usual concealed contempt for her boss. Father Bloom was the only one in the Main Building who seemed unaware of the fact that his position as chancellor had been created to draw off criticism from the president and provost, who retained all real power. Her own title was administrative assistant, but this was a nominal inflation — a titular uplift, to use the expression Harold had devised; her salary rose a cubit, a biblical least amount, again according to Harold. It was Harold's delight — to her guilty pleasure — to winkle out of her everything that should be kept confidential in her dealings with the chancellor. It was like being seduced and the longer the resistance the surer the capitulation. Harold was in computers.

"Not literally," he added.

"Virtually?"

"Good, good." He had first arrived in the chancellor's sumptuous suite in answer to a plea for help with one of the computers.

"Where is the patient?"

She took him to it as if she were the receptionist not the senior girl; she was already fascinated by him. The tenor of the office was so dull that anything out of the way qualified as interesting. Harold had not yet taken a fully interested look at her, and she was determined that this visit would rise above the impersonal. The impersonal could be had by phone, letting someone in the computer center talk you through the problem. Now that a flesh and blood human being had answered the appeal, Anita wanted a flesh and blood exchange.

Was Harold dressed casually or not? Perhaps it was the way he was so at ease that made his clothes look more comfortable than they might be. He wore real shoes, which in the age of gym shoes was a plus. His slacks were pleated and cuffed and cordovan red shoes showed beneath them. The sport jacket he wore was shapeless, black to his trousers' light brown. His eyes when he finally looked directly at her were green.

"I'll send you a replacement." He had spent two minutes examining the defective computer.

"That bad?"

"They're like Kleenex."

"Oh, I think we got more than one use out of that."

"Tissue," he said, leaning toward her, and

114

for a mad moment she thought he had said something else. "Undoubtedly one of the marvels of science, but quite up to the computer. We have some that last months."

"Kleenex?"

He was kidding, of course, though his expression did not change. But the green eyes watched, perhaps to see if she were dumb and didn't get it.

"A tanner will get you ten."

His expression changed.

"Shakespeare," she said.

"Of course."

"You're faking."

The green eyes twinkled. "The graveyard scene, first or second digger."

"You're not faking."

"I never do."

Yes, he would like coffee, and yes, they wasted forty-five minutes performing those intricate steps in an unlearned rite that might lead on to more. There was no wedding ring on his finger. Early thirties, she guessed. Whatever he gave as his age she would give as hers. Such minor obstacles as a difference in age must not stand in the way. He said he had been with the university ten years.

"Me too."

"You must have begun as a child."

"Twenty-two."

"Making you my age."

"Thirty-two?"

"Just."

"I don't know how just it is. You're a Libra, I suppose."

"What's that?"

She explained. He was. Their whatchamacallit was not in themselves, but in their stars. She didn't test him with the correct lines.

"You better get back to the computing center."

"I shall return."

"But nothing else is broken."

"To replace your ill machine."

Halfway out, he turned and came back. "How did you get the top job so young?"

"Pull."

He nodded, waved, and left.

Her father had been in accounting and Anita was never sure if his seniority, and the respect in which he was held, had smoothed the way for her. But she was good, very good, at what she did, she knew that, so pull or no pull she was on her own.

Kidding around with Harold, then going out with him, to games, to sports bars, to the opera when it arrived downtown, and to music in the Snite — Harold did not pall — compromised her unearned reputation as one of the campus feminists. This status had been

116

conferred upon her by Professor Trepani, who simply assumed that any single woman was seething with resentment against the treatment she had received from males and burned with the desire to avenge her sex.

"I'm not sure I answer that description."

"We all do."

"If you say so."

Perhaps Trepani — "Call me Trepani" — had picked up from men the knack of not listening to what others said. She was pretty good at it. That is how Anita became a certified feminist. There seemed no reason to tell Harold all that. Trepani was now aflame over the boy who had danced half naked around the field during halftime on Saturday.

"We all are." Her eyes half closed and her teeth lifted from her lower lip. "What courage that took, to defy eighty thousand people and force them to see the truth."

"The bare truth."

"For a century and a half this university has been living a lie."

"Slightly longer. 1842."

They might have been in separate telephone booths talking to different people.

"How could the rest of us not have asked that question? All it needs is asking and the answer is there."

"What's the question?"

117

"He's been arrested." Trepani seemed to have become aware of her again.

"Yes."

"Good."

"I thought you admired him."

"Do you think he took that enormous risk only to be dismissed as a prankster?"

"I don't know him."

"Nor do I. The university must bring charges against him."

"The faculty senate would go up in smoke."

"I am here on behalf of the senate. We want that boy persecuted, martyred. It's what he would want."

"Because he insulted the university?"

"Ha!" She could have blown out a match on the other side of the room. "You understand what we expect of you?"

"Tell me."

"You must ensure that the administration insists that this boy be prosecuted."

"They always do what I tell them to."

"We're counting on that."

Trepani thought she had been serious. For someone convinced of the downtrodden condition of woman, she attributed awesome power to Anita.

"What will happen to that boy who ran around the field at halftime?" Harold asked.

"He's already been arrested."

"Will they press it?"

"They better."

This surprised Harold. In any case, it would make her seem invincible to Trepani and the rest of the sisters, as Trepani called them.

"I don't think I have a vocation," Anita had said.

Vocation, vocal, voiced — unheard.

Harold asked, "I suppose they think he's tied up with the other things?"

"I suppose." Anita hadn't thought of that. Her mind was going. No wonder the chancellor was so uncharacteristically vehement. He was still brooding over his kidnapping, as who wouldn't be.

"Maybe I should go out and run around on behalf of the white settlers."

She dipped her head and looked at him through her lashes. "What would you wear?"

"My people go way back, you know. My great-great-great-grandparents were killed by Indians."

"Around here?"

"Oh no. That's why my great-great-grandfather moved here. He hated Indians."

"No wonder."

"So do I. It runs in the family." After a long pause, the corners of his mouth dimpled. "Cleveland Indians."

She punched his arm.

"That's where they came from, my ancestors."

"Was Cleveland there then?"

"We were."

17

Arthur Ballast's office was posh. The surfaces of tables gleamed, the carpet was plush and seemed to absorb sound. Telephones rang almost mutely. Green leather chairs under the pale light of lamps. Ballast's receptionist sat motionless at her desk, wearing a fixed smile, bored to death. Phil sank into a chair, crossed one long leg over the other, and rested his chin on the hand that angled toward it. Once he'd had offices in Manhattan, not as ostentatious as these, but meant to convey to potential clients that business is good but I may be able to fit you in. Roger knew that Phil did not regret putting all that behind. The move to Rye had been inspired. They also got lower insurance rates. But for all the people who telephoned from around the country knew, seeking the aid of Knight Brothers Investigations, it was to such an office as this they called. Such a call had come yesterday.

"You can't go away during football season."

Phil had laughed. "Or basketball or hockey,

and the baseball team looks good this year. Anyway, this was a local inquiry."

"Will you take it?"

"Let's talk about it after we report to Ballast. That should fulfill our commitment to the university."

Roger had told Phil what he had learned from talking with Orion Plant, and what he had inferred, and he was content to let Phil pass it on to Ballast. The little lawyer did not quite smack his lips, but it was clear that he relished this information.

"This is more than enough." He smiled eagerly at Phil first, then Roger. "The idea, you see, is to be able to tell him. 'So's your old man' if his lawyer starts making threats against the university."

"What kind of threats?"

"Well, they're talking about injustice done Plant. He was thrown out of the history department, you know."

"I heard."

"Years overdue. There is no possible case."

"So what then."

"The land. Ownership. Indians. Were you at the game Saturday?"

Phil said that he had been.

"You have to see something like that to know what fanatics they are."

"Do they have a case?"

Ballast smiled an evil smile. "I am making a novena that they think they have."

Phil rose. "Do you want a written report, a record of expenses?"

Ballast's mouth dropped open. "But you're not done."

"What else did you have in mind?"

"I want evidence that he was in on the kidnapping. The log chapel incident too, if you can manage it, but the kidnapping is the thing."

Phil agreed, and Roger wished he hadn't. Too much of the investigation would call him into play. On the other hand, he was glad to see Phil at work again. Sometimes he feared his older brother would atrophy in this undemanding existence. Phil was increasingly reluctant to go to distant cities to investigate for a client. Better local work than none.

"I guess that settles what I will do about that telephone inquiry."

"What was it all about?"

"A very enigmatic message. But I don't think devised to get me interested. A careful call."

"Now I'm interested. Who was it?"

"He gave his name as Ivray. Harold Ivray."

18

From her bedroom window in the back of the house, Laverne could look out over Cedar Grove as the Brontë girls had stared out at the great gravestones in the churchyard at Haworth. Sometimes she felt like Heathcliff's wife, abandoned for another, and sometimes like Jane, wooed and won and then robbed of happiness by the married status of her lover. It was easier fitting herself into these roles than making Orion into a Heathcliff. She knew her father's estimate of him and knew that in another world she would share it. But she was a woman and caught in the web of her feelings, helpless against them, not wanting to break the bonds.

She stared out at an old sycamore that rose above other trees. Its trunk was pied, a few of its great flat leaves still clung to the branches. The wind that had blown all night and half the day had stripped the trees of their leaves. Soon she would be diverted by the sight of the sexton and his crew raking them up and carting them away. A life spent tending the dead.

The sexton's name was Willowby; it was a hereditary job, passed on from generation to generation in his family, stretching back to the earliest settlers. He had shown her the plots her father had bought, in the new section. Laverne preferred the trees bare, they suited her valedictory mood. It had been a month since she had decided to commit suicide.

It seemed the one thing she could do now, the only statement she could make. Her love was doomed. Once, only her parents seemed to stand in her way. Then came Orion's defection to Marcia. Now Laverne sensed that she might lose Orion again. It was wrong but justifiable, she thought, to have welcomed him back into the house despite his wife. It all seemed so simple when they sat once more in the family room as they had done before. His marriage meant nothing. She clung to him as to her destiny. However infrequently, however secretively, they would meet, and she could live for that. She was capable of doing anything Orion asked. Tip over gravestones, desecrate graves? Of course. And out the back door they had gone and into Cedar Grove, and for days Laverne had nursed her secret knowledge. The madness seemed to seal her renewed love for Orion.

But she had underestimated her father.

What he had engineered was both irrevocable and devastating to any future Laverne had looked forward to involving Orion in whatever measure. Her father had not told her what he had done but Orion had. He had not told Marcia. However, confiding in her had brought him closer. It was as if he were trying to suppress the knowledge in order to continue his great campaign against the university. He had been expelled. He was no longer a doctoral candidate. He would never join the faculty of a college and live the life her father had lived. Laverne would have moved to wherever he did, willing to settle for whatever she could get. But he had been thrown out of the program. She had no doubt it was her father's doing. He had always risen to Orion's defense before. Now he had abandoned him for despicable reasons. He had become passive when Orion came back, and they had laughed and joked as before, but he must have decided then what he would do.

Even in her despair she was at Orion's beck and call. She had willingly accepted the assignment to hire a fellow to demonstrate on the field at halftime. Orion had insisted on secrecy and she had tried to comply. But how can a complete stranger hire a complete stranger for such a thing? She had hired

Bernie, the brother of a girl she worked with in the library.

"Someone from the opposing team asked me to arrange it."

"A player?" Bernie asked.

"No, a fan."

She was having second thoughts. Bernie was employed in the most menial of tasks in the library. He was not exactly retarded, but he would never qualify for Mensa. Once he understood what he must do, he became excited. She cautioned him that this must be a secret. The fan who was hiring him insisted on that.

"I don't want anything happening to you."

"Like what?"

"I think he's a gangster."

"I don't care."

She told Orion she had hired someone in Niles, a boy she had never seen before and would never see again. He might have acted more grateful. That softened her regret that she had not followed his instructions exactly.

Everyone knew that the demonstrator would be dragged from the field by security. Maybe they would put him in a room for a while, then usher him out of the stadium. No one expected an arrest.

"How much did you tell him?" Orion asked when he telephoned. He seemed to be speaking through a handkerchief.

"Where can we meet?"

"We can't."

"There are things you ought to know."

"About what?"

"I am not gong to tell you on the telephone."

She put down the phone and went back to her library tasks. She had checked and learned that Bernie was not at work. His sister Shirley drew a chair up to Laverne's desk.

"Have you heard about Bernie?"

"What?"

"Didn't you see the picture in the paper?"

Laverne just looked puzzled, waiting. Shirley leaned forward and whispered, "It was Bernie. They've arrested him. He says someone hired him to do it. Someone had to put him up to it. You know Bernie."

"I think I met him once."

Bernie was no threat, Laverne was sure of that. But when Orion called again, minus the handkerchief, they arranged to meet in the computer cluster on the second floor. Orion was worried about Bernie, not that he knew his name. Laverne fed his worry. She might tell him some details, then again she might not.

He didn't show up. She had left work early

because she wanted to sit at this window and look out at Cedar Grove and imagine she was in Haworth, star-crossed in love like all the Brontë girls.

19

Orion had never quite trusted Bartholomew Leone and now he distrusted him. It was clear that the lawyer was involved in some campaign of his own and that the dossier Orion had compiled merely represented munitions for this private battle. After he left the lawyer, Orion betook himself to a saloon some streets away from the building that housed Leone's office. It was the moment for a thorough examination of the status quo.

With a scotch and water, mixed, he repaired to a booth out of the traffic and notice of the bar. He placed his glass carefully on the surface before him and then fished from his pocket a handful of slips he had pocketed when he was last in the library. They were set out for the note-taking of those consulting the computerized holdings of Hesburgh Library and thus were there for the taking, so he took, perhaps presciently anticipating this moment. He uncapped his ballpoint, sipped his drink, and did not write, but thought.

First, women. He was like Buridan's ass

midway between two not very appetizing bales of hay. Starving would not have been a disaster, but he had lived a double life too long for assured continued safety. Laverne had come first, she had that unarguable claim; Marcia had thrust herself upon him and, far from resisting, he had taken her to his bosom. He still marveled at the shrewdness that had prompted him to urge a fast and judicial wedding upon her. He had told her of the long lines of aspirants for both Sacred Heart and the log chapel. Of course, every residence hall had a chapel and priests were thick on the ground, but fortunately that did not occur to Marcia. Besides, she was not a Catholic. He was not much of one himself, but he had the presence of mind to realize that a time might come when the nonexistence of his marriage in the eyes of the Church might be a powerful Pharisaic card to play. He had not married Marcia with any till-death-do-us-part intention, so that the marriage would have been a candidate for annulment even if it had been a Church wedding.

But what precisely was his present complaint against Marcia? She retained her job, they lived in a house that belonged to her family — to her mother, actually, who had decamped to San Diego to be with her son. Orion had been almost shocked by this dispersal of the last vestiges of a family whose roots were deep in northern Indiana. But he was happy to have his mother-in-law out of her house. Marcia was, if not a quiz kid, loyal. Nor was she as unobservant as he had supposed. Somehow she had learned of the re-established lines of communication with Laverne. Her pathetic effort to play the jealousy card by insisting on the inclusion of Byers almost endeared her to him.

Laverne. How think of her apart from her paternal parent? For years he had been grateful to Ranke for his protection, even while despising him for so violating the clear rules for the completion of the dissertation. And how think of Ranke's protection apart from Laverne? The professor was securing a husband for his daughter, that was his clear motivation. It puzzled Orion that he had jeopardized all that for Marcia.

But the yo-yo movements between the two women were nothing compared to the fundamental aim of his life, one that had taken gradual shape over the years until now it was more compelling than anything else — his future as a graduate student, his risible marriage, the plangent Laverne. Count that as Marcia's most precious endowment, the records of the Younger enterprise. He held back from Leone, excluding from the dossier that which now, in this dark moment when his present was as parlous as his future, seemed his trump. It was a story he had pieced together patiently from the initial hints until all the pieces had suddenly come together like steel filings under the influence of a magnet. The time had come to release this bombshell, if only to blast himself free of the suffocating advocacy of Leone.

He left his half-finished drink and sought a phone. The instrument had known hard service in this locale. Who knew how many drunken conversations it had transmitted — pleas, threats, cajoling, amorous cooing? The directory was similarly abused. He found the number in the Yellow Pages and dialed with the precision of a terrorist setting the timer of a bomb.

"Maudit, please."

"What department?"

"He's a reporter."

"Is he now? Does he have a first name?"

Orion could not remember Maudit's Christian name, insofar as he was a Christian. He had been the terror of the *Observer* during his senior year, a chuckling nihilist who had leveled one irresponsible charge after another at the administration, the publication for which he wrote, his fellow students, and, of course, the faculty. Orion had wheedled a savage attack from Maudit as a hedge against mistreatment.

"What is your name, please?" he demanded.

"You want my name? Who is this?"

"I am calling with the story of the half-century. If you delay me further I shall want to know your name."

"One moment."

But it was five minutes before the flutey voice of Maudit was heard. "Who is this?"

"Orion Plant."

"A voice from the grave. My own, I mean." Maudit had not survived to graduation. "What's up?"

"I intend to make your name as a journalist."

"That's good of you," came the sarcastic reply.

"I am at the Amber. In a corner booth. I shall expect you."

He hung up. He knew Maudit. The advertised worshiper of fact and objectivity was a prey to romantic unlikelihood. He would come.

He came. Twenty minutes later. The past three years had been kind to Maudit, sartorially speaking, but his face looked ravaged with lack of sleep and surplus of misbehavior. His weak eyes got used to the dim light and the thunder clouds of smoke that rolled through the Amber Saloon. He slid into the seat across from Orion.

"What are we drinking?"

"Whatever you like." He hailed an unshaven waiter and Maudit ordered.

"Now then."

"Wait until he has come and gone."

"Is it true that you have been ejected from the history department?"

"Who told you that?"

"Have you?"

"A misunderstanding. As I suggested on the phone, I have a story for you."

It might have been a lecture, it fell so neatly into place. In a few quick strokes, he recreated the primitive community that had been here prior to the arrival of Father Sorin. He spoke with real feeling of the Indians.

"Weren't they all driven away?"

"The principal tribe. A few were left, half breeds, those who wandered in afterward and stayed."

"So?"

"Approximately nineteen Indians were slain in a period of five years."

Maudit had the gift of paying attention. Orion told him of the evidence he had gathered. He knew who the killer was.

"I think the statute of limitations must have

135

run out. To say nothing of the killer."

"This is a moral matter!" Orion regained his composure. "The story has never been told. It must be told now."

"You say you have evidence."

"When I produce it, will you write the story?"

"If it holds water."

The bargain thus struck, Orion had another scotch and water. The consternation this revelation would cause Leone was only one of its charms. The main target remained the main target. This story of the serial killer, along with the doubts that could be raised about the legitimacy of the university's title to its land, would have a cumulative impact. With Leone he had spoken of compensation. Of course the lawyer took him to mean money. Well, if there was money to be had, he would take it, but there were deeper, more satisfying compensations. Even in his elation, Orion did not think of what he was doing as revenge.

20

"I've seen them together. In the library. It's all like it was before . . ."

"He has to use the library."

"Marcia." Scott Byers looked at her with tragic sympathy. Scott said he loved her; he pestered her to death, threatening to carry her off where Orion could never find them, but he left her cold. Scott was right about Orion. He walked all over her and she kept coming back for more. Of course she blamed it on Laverne.

The only reason she had told Orion about Scott Byers was that he insisted on telling her all about Laverne, the daughter of his professor, as if he were trying to say what he had put aside for her. He said all this with undisguised regret, as if she were to blame for thwarting his life. How could she keep quiet about Scott in such circumstances? Orion had feigned disinterest.

"He's a graduate student too. In mathematics."

Orion began to refer to him as X, the Unknown Quantity, as if he didn't believe her. But the time he came into the Huddle and found her having a coffee with Scott during her break, he saw that X was real. Seeing them together, Orion came and stood beside the table with an odd expression on his face as he looked down at the seated Scott. Scott looking up at him as if he were a waiter interrupting a conversation. Marcia could see that, objectively speaking, Scott was by far the better looking. When he got up to shake Orion's hand he was a head taller. He left them, husband and wife, but Orion took a different chair from the one Scott had sat in.

"Who's he?"

"I've told you about him."

"The loser?"

"If you're the winner."

He laid his hand on hers, and emotion swept over her. Orion was not a demonstrative man, and she really didn't ask much. The feel of his claiming hand on hers wiped away any remote feelings of regret she might have had talking again with Scott.

"I don't want him bothering you."

"Don't worry."

"Worry? No, I won't worry."

How swiftly he changed, one moment almost tender, the next threatening. Even so, the point she had wanted to make had been made, and by accident. He had Laverne in his past, she had Scott. She said to him then,

"And I don't want Laverne bothering you."

"Who's Laverne?" His hand returned to hers.

He had been curious about Scott. He looked him up and got to know him a bit. Marcia heard this from Scott himself. Scott thought Orion was nuts about the Indian stuff and maybe he was, but it had become an obsession with him. When he included Laverne in his big campaign, she asked Scott to come along. Orion seemed to think he had asked Scott to come. He had certainly filled his ear with his theories. During their infrequent conversations, she and Scott went into the student lounge, out of the Huddle. It would look worse if Orion came upon them there, but he never did. It was there that Scott gave her the shock of her life.

"What else does he have?" Scott asked. They had been talking of the series of incidents that had been put in motion by Orion. Scott had not been involved in meeting the chancellor's plane and at the time he had felt awful about it, but his candidacy orals of course took precedence. Marcia had the feeling now he was glad he hadn't taken part.

"What do you mean?"

Scott looked at her, then looked away. "Sometimes I've wondered what I would have done with my life if I'd been cut out of the doctoral program."

"But you passed your orals."

He was looking directly at her now. "What is Orion going to do?"

"Do? What he's always done."

"Good God, hasn't he told you?"

"Told me what?"

He had not imagined that it would fall to him to give her the news that her husband had been dropped from the graduate program in history. Orion was out. His academic career was finished. Marcia stared at Scott. Would he have made up such a thing? But she knew it was true. Little things Orion had done lately, things he'd said, now made sense as they had not before. She rose from her chair. Scott tried to take her hand, make her stay, but she wrenched free and ran back into the Huddle. She locked herself in the Ladies and stared at the featureless panel before her. It was blank as her mind, blank as her soul. Worse than Orion's expulsion was the fact that he had kept it from her for a week.

She told the manager she was ill and had to go home. It was all she could do not to quit then and there, walk away from the Huddle as Orion had to walk away from history. She put on her coat, pulled its hood over her head, and went outside, walking toward the library. The concourse of the library offered protection from the weather and did not divert her from her destination. She had been walking swiftly as if she were trying to escape from the shattering news that Scott had given her. Now suddenly she felt near collapse. She managed to get to one of the benches in the concourse, sliding across its smooth surface because of the way she had almost fallen on it. She sat there like an alien from another world while students went in and out of the automatic doors to the library.

She did not really belong here. She only worked here. She had been raised in the shadow of the university, it had haunted her life, but it was strange to her, she had little sense of its inner workings. Orion had talked endlessly about his graduate work, joined by fellow students, and Marcia had listened. What was clear was that Orion was engaged in an apprenticeship which would qualify him to spend his life as a college teacher. That was what drove him, and the others. His ambition defined their married life. Marcia had had no intimation that Orion was in trouble. He grumbled about everything, the professors, the chair, the director of graduate studies — but they all did that. It was the way she and the others complained about the management in the Huddle. Orion had been fired. But what exactly did it mean?

As if in a dream, she watched the automatic doors open and Orion come through them. He did not see her at first and nothing in his manner would have told her that Scott's story was true. Then he saw her. He stopped as if he meant to disappear inside again, but then he came toward her.

"What are you doing here?"

"I don't feel well. I'm going home."

He considered this, frowning. He looked at his watch. She waited.

"Can you get home alone all right?"

"I just saw Scott Byers."

His frown deepened. He looked around and seemed to decide this wasn't the place to repeat his warning. He still had not commented on Scott's presence on Saturday when they had watched the halftime interruption on television.

"He told me that you've been thrown out of the history program."

Orion grabbed her elbow, pulled her to her feet, and began to propel her at a great rate toward the eastern exit. Students turned to look as they hurried past. His grip had slipped to her upper arm and he squeezed it painfully. At the door, he used her as a runner uses a blocker, slamming her body against the bar and through the door. Outside, he steered her to the marble ledge that surrounded the li-

142

brary and sat her on it.

"What the hell has Scott been telling you?"

"Is it true?"

"I told you to stay away from him."

"Are you out of the graduate program?"

He struck her, with his open gloved hand, and her head snapped back. She felt the taste of blood in her mouth. He looked ferociously at her, as if he wanted to kill her, to silence her, to get rid of her questions. Marcia leapt to her feet and ran diagonally across the grass toward the bus stop. She did not even pause when she got to the road but went on to the parking lot, oblivious of the horns that blared at her. She did not care if she was run over. She didn't care about anything. Her lip had begun to swell as if she had been given novocaine, and the taste of blood persisted.

When she unlocked the front door she had little memory of how she had gotten there. She was sobbing and her face felt misshapen. Inside, she bolted the door and fell weeping on the living room couch, not even bothering to take off her coat. What Scott had told her meant nothing now. Orion had struck her, in public, had hustled her out of the library as if she were an intruder, and then had hit her there when anyone might have seen. She shriveled under the remembered humiliation. She made herself as small as possible and

143

tried to think of nothing at all.

How much later the pounding on the front door began she could not have said. She sat up immediately, terrified. If he would hit her in public, what would he do to her here? She was on her feet, thinking of escaping out the back way. As she crept past the front door, she heard a voice. She stopped. Scott? She rushed to the door and opened it, then fell back. Orion came in and looked at her strangely. "What's wrong with you?"

She moved away from him, cowering. Something almost like tenderness came into his face. He took her trembling and half hysterical in his arms.

"You hit me!"

He held her close, nodding his head. After a time, when she was calm, he eased her away and looked at her face. Slowly he lowered his lips to her swollen mouth.

21

Torsion, from the Notre Dame Foundation, the department of the administration responsible for amassing the giant endowment that had put the university far out in front of other Catholic institutions and among the top handful of all universities, was not a man inclined to rest on his laurels. Or at the moment on his backside. He paced the waiting room outside the chancellor's office as if to emphasize the importance of this unscheduled appointment. The call he had received from Tulsa allowed for no delay. And then the chancellor was standing in the door of his office, breathing through his mouth, looking warily at Torsion.

"What is it, Xavier?"

Torsion lifted a finger to his lips to stop the chancellor from saying anything and together they went into his office. Torsion pulled the door shut.

"I have just received a call from Schippers. Tulsa," he added quickly, lest the chancellor not remember. "Oil. Schippers Hall. A half-million-dollar pledge in the current drive to be doubled as our goal is neared to a maximum of five million dollars."

"Of course I know who Schippers is."

"He wishes to see you this afternoon."

"But you said he called from Tulsa."

"On the way to the airport to board his jet. He has business in Chicago and then will come on here."

The chancellor remembered Schippers's remark that the university really should have its own Lear jet. If only he had acted on that before the Hong Kong trip. A glint came into the chancellor's eye. He would mention a university Lear when the kidnapping came up, as it surely must.

"I hope you assured him I was unharmed."

Torsion looked at the nominal chief officer of the university in all its many divisions and departments and far-flung enterprises, its property in all the foreign cities where Notre Dame students spent a year abroad, its television and filming activities, the ever-growing marketing of apparel with the university's logo. Notre Dame was a big business as well as a university, and the chancellor was in charge of it all. Up to a point. What CEO can know every detail of his organization? True, true, but Torsion considered the Notre Dame Foundation as the sine qua non of everything else. Without the generosity of donors . . . He did not want to think of it.

"He wants to talk about Indians."

"Good Lord."

"I took the liberty of telling him you would see him at three."

The chancellor called in Miss Trafficant, the unflappable. Of course she could fit in a man who had given an aggregate of fifty million dollars to the university.

"What had been scheduled at three?"

"The dean of the arts school."

"No problem. No problem at all."

"Father," Torsion said, "I would like to be here when you talk to Schippers. Of course I will bring him from the airport."

"Take Johnny."

"Please," added Miss Trafficant, but only Torsion seemed to hear.

And so it was arranged. The dean of arts and letters, who had been preparing for weeks to lay before the chancellor the absolute necessity of a budget increase for his college, would be rescheduled.

Schippers, when he came, wore an expression that combined a smile and a frown. He advanced toward the chancellor and his hand shot out so abruptly that the chancellor jumped back.

"What's the matter, Father?"

147

"I am still shaken from . . . have you heard?"

"I have been hearing all sorts of things."

"I was kidnapped."

The words tumbled from Father Bloom's mouth as he told of being taken into custody when he arrived at the airport after a long trip that had taken him first across the Pacific and then on to Chicago and South Bend. "I was held captive."

"But they let you go."

"I didn't know they would at the time."

"Indians," Schippers said. "What's all this about Indians?"

"I think they may have been behind my kidnapping."

"But what's behind all these pranks?"

"I did not consider being kidnapped a prank."

"No, it's a federal offense. Ever since the Lindbergh baby. I saw the incident at halftime."

Schippers was then told of the desecrations in Cedar Grove, of the disruption of a wedding at the log chapel, Father Burnside held captive within.

"Another kidnapping, in effect. What are you doing about it?"

"Private detectives have been hired."

"Good, good."

"Philip Knight."

"Very good. I've met him. This is rotten publicity, Father. It must be taken care of at once. I suppose it's students."

The chancellor rang Miss Trafficant and asked her to have Ballast come to his office at once. Ballast came. He reported more to Schippers than the chancellor.

"We suspect a graduate student, a former graduate student. He was recently dropped from the graduate school."

"Has he been arrested?"

"There may be an indirect way of handling this. Quid pro quo. The incidents stop or we insist on prosecution."

"Do you think that should be a matter of choice?"

"We don't want to prolong the problem."

"Is there anything to the charge that the university does not have clear title to its land?"

Ballast made a noise before speaking. "Nonsense. Complete nonsense."

Schippers looked from the chancellor to Ballast and back again. He did not seem reassured. Miss Trafficant entered with a newspaper. She passed it wordlessly to the chancellor. He glanced at it, then began to read, sitting forward in his chair, a stricken expression.

"What is it?"

The chancellor ignored him, continuing to read. "My God."

It was a story of the early days of the university, of the mysterious deaths of a dozen Indians over the space of a year. Each had been strangled, then scalped. The university was mentioned in every other sentence, though there was nothing more than the locale to warrant this. Most of the bodies had been found along the Saint Joseph River. Sources had told the reporter that there was evidence the murderer had been one Jacques Cruelle, one of the original families. He was buried in Cedar Grove, not far from the grave of Pokagon that had recently been desecrated. Links were suggested rather than asserted. The story ended with a narration of all the recent episodes that seemed part of a campaign to draw attention to the questionable manner in which Father Sorin had gained possession of the land on which Notre Dame stood.

"Maudit," said Ballast, squinting in thought. "A former student. He wrote for the *Observer.*"

Schippers sent his eyes over the story with the speed reading that made underlings stand in awe of him.

"I think it is time for some arrests."

"Ballast," the chancellor said with sudden resolution, "call the police."

"That could be a mistake."

"Call them."

Back in the outer office, Anita Trafficant was surprised not to find Harold there. He had been with her when Cedrics of PR had come in with the newspaper account, telling her the chancellor must know of this at once. Of course she read it first, aloud, with Harold listening. Now he had gone. He had listened with a stony expression when she read the story and she had been sure he would want to discuss it. Anita felt let down. It was difficult to enjoy the chancellor's pile-up of problems if she had no one to discuss them with.

22

It was the long-established policy of the South Bend Police department to cooperate with the university in every way. The mayor had asked Chief Kocinski after the kidnapping of the chancellor what he intended to do about it.

"They want us to lay off."

Mayor Lessing expressed surprise. "Lay off a kidnapping?"

"I suppose they think it's students."

"Cedar Grove Cemetery is arguably within our jurisdiction. There is no doubt about the airport. We will be blamed, Boleslaw, whatever we do, but I would rather be blamed for doing something."

"What?"

"Until you investigate, that's hard to say."

"They hired Philip Knight to investigate."

"That would not exonerate us."

"You know how they can be out there."

Lessing was a graduate of Purdue and harbored an animus against Notre Dame that dated from his student days. It had been suppressed when, after his election, he was accorded royal treatment by the university. But he had an electorate to answer to. With the flight of industry, Notre Dame had become the area's largest employer, and that meant a city full of employees with the usual grudges.

Kocinski's phone rang and he ignored it until the mayor suggested he answer. It was Ballast. He listened, grunting. "Okay. Will do." He hung up. "That was the university counsel. They want us to commence an investigation."

Lessing was relieved. Duty and diplomacy had converged. He left as if he were leading in the returns and the votes from the west side had not yet been reported. Kocinski prepared to drive to the campus, taking Lieutenant Stewart with him. Stewart, whose name was Francis, was called Jimmy and he headed the detective division. He was a lanky man with a cadaverous face who chain-smoked, having taken up the habit again when a clownish attorney general had provided reason to doubt all the warnings about tobacco. Kocinksi put him in the picture on the drive.

"Sounds like a matter for student affairs."

"They've asked us to investigate."

"They got any ideas?"

"Ballast thinks they know who's behind it all."

At Ballast's office they were given an excited report of what the Knight investigation had turned up. A student named Orion Plant was the ring leader.

"A former student."

"Is he still around?"

"This is his address."

"Good," Kocinski said, when he took the slip of paper. "He lives off campus."

The address lay east of the campus in a once unfashionable area that had been known as Dog Patch, but which had become upscale with the building of the new golf course and the movement of graduate student housing along Bulla Road. The house was an old one. As they approached, Kocinski kept an eye out for dogs. He hated dogs. Dogs seemed to smell the fear he felt and went for him in preference. His leg tingled in anticipation of canine canines nipping at him. But they arrived at the door without event. Jimmy pulled open the storm door and pounded on the inner door.

"See if there's a back exit," he advised, but Kocinski stayed beside him on the steps. There could be a pack of dogs behind the house, straining at leashes that would give way easily. Jimmy pounded again, then started down the steps. "I'll go in back." But the front door opened then, after a turn of the key, a slipping of bolts, and the rattle of chains. A frightened woman looked out at them.

"Orion Plant," Jimmy said without preamble.

"He isn't here."

Jimmy ignored this and pushed inside. Kocinski followed, pulling the door shut after him. And then the thought of a dog in the house stopped him.

"You Mrs. Plant?" Jimmy asked.

"I told you, he isn't here."

"Then you won't mind if we look around."

Kocinski kept close to Jimmy as he looked into the first-floor rooms. At the stairway, he asked if there was a basement.

"You won't find him here."

"Check the basement, Chief."

"Let's stick together."

"He could get away while we're upstairs."

"I'll go up there." Who would keep a dog on the second floor?

There were three bedrooms, one with an unmade bed, and a bathroom that looked a mess. He joined Jimmy downstairs. The head of detectives lounged in a chair.

"Where is he?"

"I don't know."

"When did you last see him?"

"Yesterday."

"He didn't come home last night?"

"He was here but he went out again."

Silence. Drama lurked behind every door. The police were constantly called to scenes of domestic trouble. Mrs. Plant wore the defiant look of a cowed wife.

"What do you want him for?"

"Maybe you could tell us that."

"Who told you?"

"I'd like it in your words," Jimmy said smoothly.

There followed a fairly incoherent story. Her husband was seeing another woman, someone he went with before they married. Yesterday he had grabbed his wife and run her out of the library. Outside, where anyone might see, he had hit her. Her face was swollen, Kocinski noticed.

"You think he might be with this other woman."

"I don't know!"

"What's her name?"

"Laverne. Her father is a professor. They live on Angela Boulevard."

Good. Another off-campus address.

A bulky woman answered the door on Angela, her eyes skeptical, her hand gripping the door as if ready to bar their way if they tried to sell her anything. It had taken three long pushes on the doorbell to bring her and

156

she seemed sure she had made a mistake until she saw Kocinski's uniform. It had been a resolution he made when he was named chief, to stay in uniform as a gesture of solidarity with the department. The door swung open and they were urged inside. She seated them graciously and waited for instructions.

"Is your daughter at home?"

"My daughter!"

"Laverne?"

"Why on earth . . ." She stopped. The uniform of officialdom, doubts she seemed to have about her daughter, sowed sudden apprehension.

"I wish Otto was here."

"The professor?" Kocinski asked.

Jimmy said, "We need to speak to your daughter."

"But she isn't here."

"Was she here last night?"

"Of course!" Mrs. Ranke was angered by this impertinence. Whatever her doubts about her daughter, they obviously had limitations.

"Do you know Orion Plant?"

"Oh my God!"

She rose, she went to phone, she dialed. "Otto, come home at once. The police are here." She hung up.

For fifteen minutes the three sat silently in

the room. A clock on the mantel got progressively more audible. The furnace went on and off. Joists creaked, wind worried the windows. Mrs. Ranke looked straight ahead, into the fireplace as it happened, her mouth firmly closed.

When Professor Ranke arrived, he brought the smell of the outside air as well as a whiff of untended perspiration. The line on his forehead when he removed his beret was damp with sweat. Kocinski had not expected him to be this old, pushing seventy at least.

"You're still teaching?" Kocinski asked cheerfully when they had identified themselves.

"What's this about Laverne?"

"We are looking for Orion Plant."

"What has he to do with Laverne?"

"His wife sent us here."

The Rankes exchanged a look. He gave her the coat and beret. "Tea," he said, and she left.

"Orion Plant was a graduate student in my department. History. He has been terminated, he is out of the program. What did his wife say about Laverne?"

"When did you last see Plant?"

He made an impatient gesture. "I must know what has been said about my daughter."

158

"Plant was locked out of his house by his wife last night."

"This concerns Laverne?"

"Could it?"

The expression of a man about to lie makes the performance pointless. But Professor Ranke had second thoughts. "My daughter slept in her bed last night." He paused, then added angrily, "Alone."

"Has she been seeing Plant?"

"Once he came here often. Then he married. He has been here infrequently since. My daughter is foolish, she is a female, but she is not an adulteress."

Well, that got it all onto the table. Jimmy got back to the point. "Tell us about Orion Plant."

He might have been dictating an equivocal letter of recommendation. Orion Plant had talent, he had done his course work, passed his candidacy exams, and was ostensibly working on his dissertation.

"He became diverted by tangents dealing with the early history of the university. His is an antic, undisciplined mind. He ran over the allotted time to write a dissertation by several years. Finally we terminated him."

"How long ago was that?"

"A week ago. Slightly more."

"What sort of tangents?"

"Indians. Native Americans," he added, as if this was being recorded. And it was, in a sense, as Jimmy had a phenomenal memory. When he wrote up his reports the typewriter never stopped clacking, as if he had composed it all in his mind as the investigation went on.

"There seems evidence that he is behind the recent incidents on campus. And off."

"I don't doubt it."

"Why not?"

"He is a resentful man. He causes himself trouble and then says that he has been treated unjustly. He thinks he has accomplished things because he has imagined them. He is a romantic. A revolutionary."

"Did he ever talk to you about Native Americans?"

"He talked of little else. It had become an obsession."

"Does he have Indian blood?"

"He is a second-generation American."

"Does your daughter work?"

Again the about-to-lie expression, and again truth won out. "In the library."

"On campus?"

"On campus."

Jimmy rose, Kocinski followed suit. Mrs. Ranke appeared with a tea trolley. Jimmy sat when he saw the chocolate cake. Mrs. Ranke poured. It might have been one of a hundred academic tea parties. Jimmy had two pieces of cake. Ranke sipped his tea and brooded. Kocinski put Mrs. Ranke in the picture.

"I always knew he was trouble."

"You fawned on him," the professor growled. "You were as bad as Laverne."

It was when they were on their way to the library that they were informed of the body that had been found near Fatima Retreat House. They headed there.

23

Father James had not had so much attention in years. With Sweeney, his superior at Fatima, he had waited in the lounge until the police came. He was still wearing his out-of-door clothes. He told them the story as they left the house and started toward the lake. Other vehicles were now parked in the retreat house lot, which had been empty, the snow not cleared away. They were low priority for snow plowing at any time, but early in the season they would be lucky to have the lot cleared before the snow melted.

Father James noted the absence of ducks as they gained the lake path. He led the way along it to the point where the ducks had wandered off it and begun to quarrel over a glove. Paramedics were already there, the call Father Sweeney had made providing directions enough for them. A young woman with a ponytail, not dressed for the weather, knelt beside the body.

"I gave him absolution," James said.

The girl looked up at the uniformed policeman Father James had led with his lanky companion to the scene. "He's dead, of course."

"How long?"

She shrugged. "Let Doyle guess."

Doyle, the medical examiner, came across the snow in street shoes, lifting his knees high as if he were in a pasture inhabited by a healthy herd. He joined the paramedics and looked down at the dead man. His eyes lifted and he looked out at the frozen lake. He glanced up at the trees. He might have been wondering why he had ever left private practice for what had seemed an undemanding sinecure. He squatted as if to line up a putt and studied the body without touching it. Then he reached out, lifted an arm, and let it drop.

"What's with the feathers?"

"He was wearing them."

Doyle began to make a repetitious noise. Tom-toms. He looked up at Jimmy. "Twenty-four hours. At most forty-eight."

"Cause of death?"

Doyle made a face and pointed to the bloody mess on the back of the man's head.

"Turn him over."

Rigor mortis had come and gone, Father James thought. He had picked up such lore from Agatha Christie, whose *opera omnia* were on the retreat house shelves. How like inert matter a dead body is, mere filling for the clothes. The lanky man leaned over the body and found a wallet. He opened it and looked at his uniformed companion.

"Well, we found him."

"Orion Plant?"

"Soon to be planted."

All the talk over the body was impersonal, jocular, a kind of verbal anesthetic to shield the speakers from the reality of death. *Requiem aeternam dona eis, domine, et lux perpetua luceat eis.* As a young man, Father James had worried about such prayers. How could a soul rest? *Locum refrigerii et pacis.* Peace, yes, but refrigeration for the soul? Such quibbles faded with the years. Faith is a mystery and few things try it as much as the dogma of the resurrection of the body. Orion Plant, when he had come upon him, looked as if he were already part of the soil. Turning him over had not helped. His face was drained of blood, making the painted streaks vivid. The medical examiner was making a tom-tom noise again.

Father James told his simple story twice there by the body. And after the body had been slid into a rubber bag and zipped up and taken away, he and Chief Kocinski and Lieutenant Stewart went back into the lounge where he told it all again. Father Sweeney kibitzed and, as was his habit, interrupted whenever possible.

"We didn't hear a thing," he said. "When was it supposed to have happened?"

Stewart looked up at Sweeney. "If you had heard something that might help set the time."

"Did you hear anything, James?"

"I take out my hearing aid at night." He looked slyly at Lieutenant Stewart. "In order to sleep soundly."

Stewart barked in appreciation. "The question presupposes that it was done here. I want another look at that site. The body could have been brought here."

"What an awful thing to do!" It was unclear whether Father Sweeney meant killing the man or bringing his body here as opposed to somewhere else.

Father James's day in the sun was far from over when the police were through with him. WNDU sent over a crew, hoping for an exclusive on a murder in their own backyard, but Maudit from the *South Bend Picayune* was hard on their heels. Father James was somewhat awed to be interviewed by a young lady he had watched on the screen for several years. She was even nicer-looking in person, and she treated him with great deference.

"I understand you gave the man the last rites."

"Instinct."

"Of course you wouldn't have known if he was Catholic."

But it turned out that he was, nominally. Married outside the Church though. It was Maudit who had such arcana. The crew packed up and left and Father James and the reporter settled down as if in an ordinary conversation.

"He had come to me, Father. We talked, had a beer."

"Would you like something now?"

"What do you have?"

Whatever he wanted. He asked for beer. Father James split it with him. The young man had seemed hesitant and James didn't want to waste the house's supplies.

"Why had he come to you?"

"He had a story. Father, I want you to know I'm a Domer, all right. But the public has a right to know."

"To know what?"

"Everything."

"Only God is omniscient."

Maudit sipped his beer, and studied the priest. "Do you read the *Picayune*?"

"Oh no."

"Why not?"

"When the students are here the *Observer* is more than I can take. I prefer television."

"Show biz," Maudit said dismissively. "I

published a story about a serial murderer who operated around here in the nineteenth century. My editor wants it to be a series, but they took care of that."

"They?"

Maudit lifted his brows significantly. "Let's just say that you stumbled on the body of my source there by the lake."

"*Fons et origo.*"

"I took German." Maudit rose. "But I wanted to take French. Maybe I will someday. Thanks for the beer."

"*Auf Wiedersehen.*"

24

Phil had begged off the dinner, wanting to get all the details on the discovery of the body of Orion Plant, so Roger dined alone with Father Carmody in the refectory of Holy Cross House.

"Some woman who works in the archives has made a list of all the murders committed on campus over the years."

Roger knew of it. "If I had been asked, I would have said none."

"I wonder if she has the names of all those Indians that were written about in this morning's paper?"

Roger made a note to check this with Whelan. The truth was, he wanted to get his mind off recent events. That his conversations with Orion Plant had led to the search for him as a suspect made him uneasy. He had not relished the thought of seeing either Plant or his wife again. Now he would not see Plant again in this life. As for Mrs. Plant, Carlotta Bacon, the wife of another history graduate student, had gone to be with her and had phoned back to graduate student housing that the new widow was hysterical. Orion had hit her in the face in public view and now she mourned him like a Neapolitan.

"We may play in the snow this Saturday."

A light but swift team from an effete California campus was due for the weekend and cold weather was thought to favor Notre Dame. Father Carmody dismissed this. "Take a look at the parts of the country our players come from. We used to be heavy with players from Pennsylvania, those that escaped the clutches of Joe Paterno, but now we seem to recruit in Dixie."

The remark prefaced one of Father Carmody's mild lamentations at the present's poor show against the past. He was the elderly darling of the administration, a useful link to the past to parade before alumni, but he disapproved of most of what they did.

"Once *Ex corde ecclesiae* would have been redundant. Now some noisy professors profess embarrassment at being Catholic theologians."

"Save in their own sense." Father Carmody needed little prodding, but Roger wanted him to go on and blot out thoughts of poor Orion Plant. The plangent litany continued, practiced, repetitious, true. Of course, Father Carmody did not realize how thoroughly Catholic the campus appeared to one coming

169

from the outside. Roger had never been in such congenial circumstances. The students were edifying, the ambience almost sacral, only some administrators seemed fitfully to hunger for the fleshpots of Egypt.

Ballast had called Roger's office to tell him his report on Orion Plant had borne fruit. "We are bringing in the police."

"But he's already been expelled."

"Well, he won't leave the area. He can be more trouble now."

"What's the charge?"

"I'll leave that to the police. They have enough to bring him in for questioning, thanks to you."

Roger felt awful. But his spirits perked up when Father Carmody began to talk about Frank O'Malley and Dick Sullivan, Tom Stritch and Tony Chroust, Joe Evans, legendary faculty members of what the priest clearly regarded as the golden age of Notre Dame, academically speaking.

"We were a college then, with the emphasis on undergraduates. Tony was the only scholar of the bunch, a bit of a pedant. He left quite a bit of money to the law school. At least it was considered quite a bit of money then. Like yourself, he was a university professor — law, history, philosophy — he taught them all. Courses that otherwise would never have been offered. Dick was a writer, a self-effacing man, and Frank was Frank, sui generis."

"Do you know Otto Ranke's book on famous authors who lectured at Notre Dame?"

"I was able to help a bit with that."

"He should write another, about Notre Dame's great faculty members."

"Talk to him about it."

"I will." It was not only a worthwhile idea, it would provide a convenient excuse to pay a call on Ranke. "Tell me about Leo Ward."

"L or R?" The two priests had been distinguished by their middle initials, taken to stand for literary and rational. "R."

"Another self-effacing man. If I have anything against him it was his insistence that we needed a graduate program in philosophy. He brought Yves Simon here."

"Was Jacques Maritain ever a faculty member?"

The old priest shook his head as if Roger should have known better. "Just a visitor, but a constant one. He loved Notre Dame. He bequeathed us his house in Princeton and his heart."

"His heart?"

"His literal heart. He died in France, though, and the medical authorities wouldn't permit the transfer."

"How extraordinary."

"Oh, I don't know. They fought over pieces of Thomas Aquinas's body. A few years ago, the then provost sold the house. Just like that. A damned fool thing to do."

Father Carmody explained that it had functioned for a time as a residence for Notre Dame faculty on leave and doing research at Princeton.

"You heard Astrik Gabriel's *mot*?"

"Tell me."

"It's a good thing we didn't get the heart. That provost would have sold it too."

Ancient faces at the other tables turned when Roger roared. Not everyone here was thoroughly compos mentis, but Father Carmody said it came on so gradually it was not always noticed. And then they got back to Saturday's game.

"Are you going, Father?"

"I may watch it on television."

"Come to our place. We'll watch it together and then have dinner when Phil gets back."

The old priest extended his hand and they shook on it. "*Deo volente,* of course."

"Of course."

25

Phil had been to the morgue to view the body and to read Doyle's report. The final judgment was that the body had been dead for less than twenty-four hours when it was discovered.

"So he would have died at what? Six, seven o'clock."

"More or less," Doyle said with the caution of his trade. He had seen what had happened to coroners and medical examiners in recent highly publicized and televised trials. "He didn't just die, he was murdered."

"Weapon?"

"A tomahawk."

"What?"

"It was found thrown into the snow six feet from the body."

"So he was killed there."

"No. He was brought there. There are signs that a vehicle of some kind was used to transport the body to the site. The weapon must have been pitched at the same time."

"A tomahawk," Phil mused. It seemed an inappropriate weapon for the self-appointed champion of Native Americans. "And he was wearing feathers."

Doyle nodded. "He was a diabetic."

"Is that relevant?"

"It probably was to him."

When Phil talked to Boleslaw Kocinski he found him somewhat nonplussed. The chief had set out in pursuit of Orion Plant as a suspect and now they were going to have to find out who killed him.

"The university was out to get him, of course. But I don't suppose any of them did it."

Phil left the remark uncommented on. He was glad when Jimmy came in and they went off together where Phil would receive a briefing.

"I looked in at the morgue."

"Someone conked him on the head, probably with his own tomahawk, and then brought the body to where it was found."

"Some one or ones?" Phil said.

"They must not have gotten out of the vehicle. There are no footprints or any other sign of people milling around."

"What kind of vehicle?"

"It could have been a lawnmower."

Phil imagined someone driving a mower along the lake path in the driving snow, Orion draped over the raised blades.

"Or a snow plow?"

Jimmy nodded. "More likely. We got some fair tire prints. I'll have someone check out the ground crew vehicles."

"I shouldn't imagine it would be all that easy to appropriate one, especially during the snowstorm."

"They didn't begin plowing the walks or university roads until morning. The place is deserted."

"I know. I live there. It will be a funny game with most of the students away."

"Who would go in this weather?"

"I would. But it's supposed to clear up. That was a freak snowfall."

"I'm due to talk to the chancellor's secretary. At her house. She can give me half an hour. She sounds like an efficiency expert. Want to come along?"

Miss Trafficant had a condo in a development on the east side of the Saint Joseph River. The place had a winter look, almost a Christmas look, with the trees pasted with snow and their branches limned with it as if with decorations. There was a light on over her door.

"I suppose our half hour has already begun."

Her coat was thrown over a chair and there

was a man watching television. Harold Ivray. He nodded and went back to the televised hockey game.

"Tell me all about the kidnapping," Jimmy said.

"Are you Professor Knight's brother?" she asked Phil. She had looked at him more closely when Jimmy identified him.

"That's right."

"He's been a great help."

Phil didn't ask how. Jimmy was waiting for her to begin.

"You'll want to talk to Father Bloom, of course, although he's still pretty shaken by the experience. His driver was on his way to pick him up at the airport and en route someone suddenly appeared over the back seat, told him to pull over, and then pressed something to his face. He went out like a light."

"I'll talk to him too."

"His name is Johnny. He's an idiot. They must have driven the car to the airport. When Johnny came to he was in short-term parking. But the car they shoved the chancellor into wasn't the university car."

"I was given the impression that the university thought it might have been Orion Plant behind it. The late Orion Plant."

"It looked that way, didn't it?"

"Looked?"

She turned to Jimmy. "My own theory was that it was done to make Johnny look like a fool."

"Hmm."

"If you talk to him, you'll see what I mean."

Johnny was in a sports bar on Route 23 with his wife Fiona, surrounded by a half-dozen giant screens bringing in athletic contests of note from around the nation. Johnny's face was needed as support for his luxurious eyebrows that made his nose seem false. His baseball cap was pushed to the back of his narrow head. Fiona loomed over him subserviently.

"We're investigating the death of Orion Plant."

"Never knew him."

"We think he's the fellow who overpowered you and took over your car."

This tore Johnny's wandering eye from the screen he had been favoring. He became animated, and profane. Fiona clung to his arm as if to keep him earthbound.

"The bastard must've been hiding in the back seat. Creepy thought, but who checks the back seat before he gets in a car? I do, that's who. That's where my passengers ride, I want it to be as it ought to be, but that day I didn't look, and see what happened? I'm lucky I didn't lose my job."

"Who would do a thing like that to you?"

Johnny entered easily into the notion that the whole episode had been contrived to embarrass him rather than the chancellor.

"I've thought about it, I've thought about it."

"What did you come up with?"

"Johnny," Fiona said in a warning purr, but he ignored her.

"There's a bitch who works in his office. Miss Traffic Cop. Half my age and she thinks she runs the place."

"You think she arranged it?"

"Johnny!"

"I'd look into it if I was you." He glared up at his wife. "I was kidnapped as much as he was."

"Who is Harold?" Phil asked Johnny.

"Harold?" The eyebrows rose dramatically in thought. He shook his head. "I don't know any Harold. Who is he?"

"You have an Uncle Harold," Fiona said.

Jimmy went through the account of the episode Johnny had given them, a marvel of pithiness. Husband and wife exchanged a glance. "I couldn't have said it better myself."

"It's just what you said."

Johnny promised any future cooperation that would be asked of him and Jimmy and

Phil left the den of cacophony and went out into the night air.

"That's it for today," Jimmy said. "Where can I drop you?"

They were not half a mile from the apartment and soon Phil was settled down before a single screen, watching a single game. How could you watch a game when you were watching another game? Other games. He was soon absorbed and was almost surprised when Roger came in on a rush of cold air. Of course he would not have heard Roger's golf cart.

"Have a good dinner?" he asked, turning back to the hockey game.

"I'll tell you all about it."

"Me too," Phil said. "Later."

"Have you eaten?"

"Lieutenant Stewart and I had a pizza."

"A snack! I'll warm up the risotto."

26

Otto Ranke had been filled with foreboding when Freda called to tell him of the police visit, and he found little reassurance in the fact that the brother of Roger Knight was also investigating recent events. Freda's account was as incoherent as the initial seminar presentation of a new graduate student, but the central fact emerged that it was Laverne they had wanted to see. She had not been home for three nights now, and when they heard of the death of Orion, Freda expressed a ghoulish elation. The demise of the faithless suitor allayed Freda's fear that their daughter had run off with the scoundrel. Apparently Orion's wife had had the same thought, and becoming a new widow had not kept her from conveying her suspicions about Laverne and Orion to the police. But how could Otto feel that the whole sordid connection was at last definitively over when he did not know where Laverne was?

He had from a distance checked her place of work in the library and seen that she was not there. Later he telephoned and in a disguised voice asked for her.

"Laverne isn't in today," he was told.

"They've killed her too," Freda wailed. "They'll find her body somewhere near." And she began to wail louder. Otto ignored her.

"Do you want to report her missing to the police?"

"They already know that. They're looking for her."

Did Freda have any inkling of what the police interest in their daughter might be? When he arrived at his office, Russell Bacon was waiting in the hallway to see him. The graduate student followed him in and this irked Ranke. He liked to be settled in before receiving visitors. Bacon shifted from foot to foot watching the professor hang up his coat and crown the stand with his hat. He settled behind his desk and looked at his visitor.

"Well, sir?"

Bacon sat down. "Laverne is staying with us. Carlotta didn't think I should tell you, but you must be frantic."

"Laverne is with you?"

"Carlotta works in the library too. They've gotten to know one another. When she came to the door the other morning, of course we took her in."

"In the morning."

"The wee hours."

Professor Ranke did not know what to say. His sense of relief gave way to anger that Laverne should have caused such anxiety to her mother, hiding in graduate student housing, so close by, while her mother imagined the worst.

"Why?"

"I've kept out of it. She and Carlotta talked for hours. I went back to bed. Apparently she intends to run away and start a new life."

The phrase was ambiguous and Ranke scowled at Bacon. This was the plagiarist who had beaten the rap, as he would doubtless have put it, brazenly submitting a paper of Orion Plant's as his own. Did the Bacon hospitality have anything to do with his old grudge against Orion for exposing him, however ineffectually? How many knew of Laverne's continued hankering after Orion despite the fact that he had unceremoniously dropped her for another? That she had resumed whatever it was with Orion after his marriage was probably better known than the doomed courtship that had played itself out in the privacy of the Ranke family room.

Bacon's flat face with its crab-apple nose and pouting lips was repugnant to Professor Ranke. That a student might under pressure cheat and plagiarize was, if not excusable, understandable. But Bacon had been under no pressure when he purloined Orion's seminar paper, nor had he felt an iota of remorse when he was confronted with the evidence of his deception. The best defense is a good offense. Bacon welcomed the official inquiry. The two papers were identical, but Orion had printed off a copy of his own paper after Bacon had submitted the paper as his own. Bacon raised the question of who had stolen from whom. Orion could not find the file on the hard drive of his computer. It had been erased. The case evaporated. But Bacon knew, and Ranke knew, the truth of the matter. And so of course had Orion, who began to call Bacon the Earl of Oxford.

"I understand you wrote Shakespeare too."

Bacon was no match for Orion's bitter sarcasm.

"You must submit the paper for the departmental prize. You may have better luck with it than I did."

This had been in the mail room of the department, before grinning witnesses. Bacon had picked up a metal waste basket and brought it down on Orion's head. The bonking sound had brought others to the scene. Orion had wrested the waste basket from Bacon and was inspecting the dent his head made. He feinted at Bacon and his assailant fled, borne along on gales of derisive laughter.

"Your nemesis is no more," Ranke said to Bacon now.

"That's an awful thing to say. Carlotta and I are having a Mass said for poor Orion."

Ranke was surprised in recent years by any allusion to religious belief on the part of his students. One no longer knew which were Catholics and which were not, and those that were understood their faith less than a band of Zulu catechumens. Little bits of legalistic lore clung to their minds, picked up God knew where. Thus, Laverne's remark that Orion had not married his wife in the Church so it really wasn't a marriage. Meaning he was no more encumbered than when he used to reign in the family room. Laverne's Mass attendance was dilatory, though Sacred Heart Basilica was closer than the library to which she loped off each weekday.

"How is Laverne taking it?"

"Orion? She was so upset when she came to us — she hasn't gotten much better — that Carlotta hasn't even told her about Orion."

"You say she came in the wee hours."

"Tuesday night. Wednesday morning, really."

Where in God's name had she been? Of course he would not ask Bacon. Any relief he felt at learning where his daughter was had been eclipsed by the humiliation of hearing this from Bacon.

"Thank you for telling me."

"I think you ought to come get her."

"Of course."

Bacon stood and waited. He meant immediately. Why had he let Ranke take off his things and settle behind the desk if this had been the purpose of his visit? But Ranke rose and put on his coat once more. Bacon helped him and Ranke resented it. He clamped his hat on his head, and indicated that Bacon should lead the way.

The freak snow had melted, leaving the campus looking drab and dull. The library rose toward an overcast sky, the colors of its massive mural even more subdued. Bacon walked beside him, not taking his arm, but seemingly on the qui vive in case the professor lost his footing on this glazed walk. Ranke glowered into the impending gloom, not encouraging his companion to talk. What lay ahead? Would Laverne throw a tantrum, providing Bacon with more gossip for his fellow students? But Laverne's taking refuge with the Bacons was damning enough.

Carlotta Bacon was letting herself out of the apartment when they arrived. She was startled to see who was with her husband.

"Oh my God."

"Carlotta, he had to be told."

"But she's gone."

"Where?" Ranke demanded.

"Where I'm going. To the library. She said it was time she got back to work."

"Did you tell her . . ."

"That's when she came around and said she was going back to work. She took it very well. Maybe I should have told her right away."

Bacon shrugged and looked at Ranke. Ranke looked at the couple and imagined what they thought of him. What nonsense had Laverne poured into their ears? He nodded in what might have been thanks, turned, and plodded back to his office.

27

With the death of his client, Bartholomew Leone had lost the weapon he had intended to use against Ballast, but he had been handed another.

"This would not have happened if you had not had him hunted down."

"Nonsense." Ballast sat smugly behind his oversize desk.

"You deny that you harassed him mercilessly?"

"Your complaint, insofar as you have one, is with the police, not me."

"You informed them. You pressured them to bring him in."

Ballast steepled his fat little fingers with their manicured nails. His class ring was prominent on his right hand, his wedding band on his left. His smile was pursed. Leone shifted field adroitly, like a Rockne back.

"Of course it will all come out now."

"What will come out?"

"The damning evidence that Orion Plant had collected about the early history of this place."

"If the lurid tale of the murder of some Indians long ago by someone unconnected with the university is a fair sample, I would urge you to make the rest public."

"You know not what you ask."

Ballast rose and laid his hand on his desk. "Is this what you came to say?"

Leone rose too. His own smile was confident if not smug. "I thought it only fair to give you warning."

"On behalf of the university, I thank you."

"I doubt that the university will thank you when I tell them that you urged me on."

"Why do you hate Notre Dame so?"

"Please do not identify your unprepossessing person with this great institution."

It was not bad as an exit line. He found his car with a citation tucked under the windshield wiper. He had parked in a spot reserved for the handicapped. It seemed half the parking spaces in the world were reserved for the handicapped, as if one were living in a recovery area for the walking wounded. He tore the citation free, crumpled it into a ball, and sent it sailing toward a receptacle. Swish. Two points. Make that three. Humming, he settled himself behind the wheel of his Lexus.

Reconstructing the visit to Ballast on the drive back to his office, Leone was satisfied that he had acquitted himself well. Not an unequivocal triumph, but then there had only been an exchange of lawyerly remarks. Arrived, he gave instructions that he was not to be disturbed save for the gravest reasons. He got out Orion's dossier and opened it on his desk, put a note pad beside it, and though he had read it, he began again to read what the scowling graduate student had brought him. He paused before beginning. May he rest in peace, he murmured, then set to work. He might have been fulfilling his client's last wishes.

The appendix of the dossier consisted of photocopies of old records, most of them from the university archives, some from the Northern Indiana Historical Society. Documentation for the charges Orion Plant had formulated in his text. His account of the displacement of local tribes and the heroic saga of Father Petit made for moving reading, but Leone found that the damning tone of Orion's narrative detracted from the facts, which were damning enough uncommented on. Deeds of transfer from the county plat books recorded the sale of the confiscated land. The trial led through Father Badin to Edward Sorin, founder of the university. As a strictly legal matter, there was, of course, no case. Leone had recognized that from the beginning. But it could easily be argued that the

189

tainted past of the land, however legally acquired, spelled a public relations disaster for the university.

Half an hour later Leone asked his secretary to put through a call to Maudit at the *Picayune*. They met in the courthouse café.

The reporter was a furtive young man whose pride in his story about the slaughter of Indians by an irate settler seemed under control.

"I caught hell for that."

"From the university?"

"Not directly. I assume they were behind it. My editor chewed me out for considering last century's events as news."

"They must have gotten to him."

"Did you see my piece this morning?"

"No."

"All about the heightened security for Saturday's game."

"Are you saying you don't care to pursue the matter?"

"It's not what I want."

"Orion gave you only the tip of the iceberg."

"Awful what happened to him."

"Are you frightened?"

"What do you mean?"

"Who do you think was responsible for his brutal death?"

"I'm not on that story."

"I'm asking you to put two and two together."

Maudit occupied himself with this arithmetical problem. "I don't get you."

"Who was hurt by your story?"

Maudit tossed back his head. "Descendants of the killer, I suppose. There aren't any descendants of that tribe still living within a hundred miles. Or beyond for that matter. I stopped trying to trace them."

Was the reporter being willfully obtuse? In any case, he was clearly no longer the means whereby Orion's research would reach a wider public. Maudit got to his feet.

"I'll be covering the funeral."

"You could mention things in that story."

Maudit shook his head. "I do not want to join the ranks of the unemployed."

The hero of a free press left and Leone was not unhappy to be rid of him. He sat pondering the situation. Making the dossier public brought it to the attention of thousands of indifferent readers. The aim was not the masses, but those who might act on it. He summoned his secretary.

"I want a dozen copies of this made," he said, handing Mrs. Atriks the dossier. The woman was crippled with arthritis but was the most efficient secretary he had ever had. But then she was the only one he had ever had. How she managed to work the keyboard of her computer with hands twisted with arthritis was a mystery. "I want copies sent to every lay member of the board of trustees of Notre Dame."

Gerry nodded.

"FedEx?"

"Of course."

And she hobbled out with her burden.

So it was that, the following day in Tulsa, Mr. Schippers scanned the contents of the package that had arrived. As he read, he felt that the chancellor had been less than frank with him about the crisis facing the university. In another letter, mailed from the chancellor's office by the hand of Miss Trafficant, was a newspaper clipping about the body found near Fatima Retreat House. Orion Plant. That name had arisen when the chancellor told him the suspicions about that student.

"Former student," he had added. "Dismissed. Doubtless this is his revenge."

But now the avenger was dead, found on the campus. He picked up the phone and asked to be put through to his colleagues on the Notre Dame board of trustees.

"Seriatim," he added.

★ ★ ★

Meanwhile, Bartholomew Leone had arranged to meet with Professor Quinlan, president of the faculty senate and a notorious malcontent.

28

Anita Trafficant called the computing center and asked for Harold. He was out on a job.

"Send him a message on his pager."

"What's the message?"

"This is Anita Trafficant in the chancellor's office."

"But that's where he said he was going."

"Then he received my message."

She hung up. It was better that he came unsummoned. Suddenly she felt in pursuit of Harold, though it had been otherwise at the beginning. She dated the change to the arrival of the police at her door just when they had been about to set off for Sunny Italy. That made no sense. Harold had shown no interest in the inquiries of the city detective and Philip Knight, the brother of the Professor of Catholic studies. Harold had gone on watching a ridiculous hockey game until the detectives had gone.

Of course she had known that the Knight brothers were private investigators in New York, despite the formidable learning of Roger that had more than justified the offer to him of the endowed chair. She had assumed that Philip had gone into virtual retirement since moving to Notre Dame. That Ballast had enlisted the aid of the brothers to find out who was behind the disturbing events of the previous week had not surprised her. She had assumed they were on a wild goose chase until Orion Plant emerged as the most likely person behind the apparent campaign to embarrass the university. It occurred to her that the death of the dismissed graduate student lifted the threat of any further harassment. Prosecuting him would have been to prolong the effect of what had already happened.

"Busy?"

Harold looked in at her, grinning.

"Of course I'm busy."

"No one would have guessed. Got any coffee?"

"I thought you came to ask me to lunch."

"You read my mind."

But his mind was just what she could not read. She had told herself that it was demeaning for her to fall for someone in the computer center, a man at the beck and call of anyone having a computer. A very good-looking maintenance man, and eligible. Who obviously liked her. His one suggestion that their relation move to a more intimate level had been rebuffed, strategically. Or tactically.

Anita Trafficant was of a mind to accept an offer of marriage from Harold Ivray.

He suggested the Decio deli, which would not have been her choice, but she was so pleased to see that his recent preoccupation and indifference were a thing of the past that she did not demur.

"You read my mind," she said.

"If only I could."

"You're not trying hard enough."

"Because I'm Hertz?"

"I don't get it."

"Number one. Avis isn't, and has to try harder."

"You're number one," she purred, and slipped her arm through his.

The deli was crowded with refugees from the library staff and a handful of resentful professors. A place designed for the faculty had become the gathering place of the help. Two secretaries leaned toward one another at the table they shared, knees touching. The sandwiches were huge and Anita offered to share with Harold, but he was hungry. They ordered one and a half turkey sandwiches and Anita took possession of the last empty table, getting to it before a shaggy, shuffling professor with greasy hair and a lowering expression could claim it. His bald companion grinned menacingly. Anita ignored them, irked that

196

they did not recognize her. No one else seemed to either. She decided that was the attraction of this place.

"Wasn't that terrible about the graduate student," she said when Harry brought their food and sat across from her, his knees touching hers as if they were secretaries. But it was just the size of the tables.

Harold frowned as if he didn't understand her.

"You have to have heard of the body found by the lake day before yesterday."

"Was he a graduate student?"

"Was is the word. He'd been expelled."

He clearly was not interested in the topic. Why should he be? Still, a murder was a murder. He began to talk about hockey.

"That's where we're going tonight."

Ye gods. "Oh good."

The fact was, she would have gone to a wrestling match with him if that's what it took. He decided that she needed a short course on the game to enhance her pleasure that night. Was it for this that they had slipped and slid across the campus? Their walk had given her added excuse to cling to him. He must be brought to a decision before he suggested staying over at her place because she didn't know if she could trust herself.

Back at the office, she settled at her desk

and ignored the work that awaited her. Father Bloom had been getting calls from trustees and was unlikely to bother her for a time. She turned to the computer and called up a database few had access to. Employees of the university, divided into categories. Would Harold be staff? He was listed under maintenance. She called up his personnel file.

A September birthday, late. But she already knew he was a Libra. She herself was a Pisces. A good combination, very good. Adams High School, a degree from IUSB. He had worked at Best Buy before being hired by the university. The data on the form would not have interested anyone, but for Anita Trafficant it was suffused with an emotional charge, conferred on it by her desire to become Mrs. Harold Ivray. She went back to the top of the form, What was his middle name?

Harold Cruelle Ivray.

Cruelle? Why was that familiar? Mrs. Harold Cruelle Ivray, she mused. And then she remembered. Cruelle was the name of the early settler written about in the story in the *Picayune*. She had sent that off to the trustees, along with the story of the finding of the body of Orion Plant. Cruelle. Funny, Harold hadn't mentioned that. She would kid him that he was the descendant of a nineteenth-century mass murderer.

29

Already on Friday the lot behind the house was beginning to fill with cars of people come for the game. Marcia welcomed the presence of strangers. People she knew, more or less, had been coming by, not knowing what to say any more than she did. Orion had not made her feel much like a wife, betraying her with the professor's daughter he swore he'd never loved and had been glad to get free of. Ha. She tried to rid herself of these thoughts, telling herself she was a widow now and to stop thinking that Orion had only gotten what he deserved. He had become fanatic about some long-dead Indians, giving them — and Laverne Ranke — the attention she deserved. Scott Byers was there most of the time now, but other people who came, the Bacons, other fellow students of Orion's, probably thought he was there for the same reason they were. People left and others came, and Scott remained and after everyone else had gone he stayed.

The first night she slept with him, wanting to be held and comforted, but doing her part too; she had felt awful until she convinced herself that she wasn't married anymore, this was different, and besides, it was a way of balancing accounts with Orion. The police had been the worst, the detective named Stewart and another man introduced as Detective Knight. That was funny, Knight, but it must have been just a coincidence. This man was tall and had the weight his height accommodated, whereas Professor Knight . . .

"He knows more than the rest of them put together," Orion had assured her.

"Well, he weighs more than the rest of them put together."

"Solid gold."

"Solid fat," she said, and Orion had drawn back his arm.

"You hit me and I'll kill you."

Among the things she did not tell the police: "He didn't come home at all that night."

Scott nodded. "She told all of us that."

"Us."

"I'm a graduate student in mathematics." He put out his hand and the man named Knight took it. Lieutenant Stewart just looked at Scott and she wished he would shut up.

"I'll be going, Marcia," Scott said at last. "If there's anything we can do . . ."

We? After he left, Marcia supposed he

hadn't wanted the police to be thinking bad things of her, having a man in the house when her husband had just been found murdered.

"Had he mentioned anyone threatening him?"

"He did the threatening."

"Oh?"

"It was the way he was. A chip on his shoulder."

"Out to get the university?"

"He said he was for the Indians, not against Notre Dame."

"How did that get started, his dissertation?"

"I guess."

"How did he feel about being let go by the history department?"

"He was mad. At first. But in a way, I think he was glad."

"How so?"

"He had been at it for years. I think it had soured for him."

They wanted to know about her, where she had met Orion, did she still work in the Huddle. It was almost a relief to talk to them, tell them anything, they seemed interested in whatever she might say.

"You were here Tuesday night?"

"Yes."

"Weren't you worried when he didn't come

home?" She had been worried he would. Scott had come by when he heard about the scene outside the library and he swore he would beat the hell out of Orion when he showed up. It was nice to have a protector, but she had wondered if Scott would be a match for Orion.

"You going to be all right here alone?" Stewart asked.

"I've lived here all my life."

"Any relatives?"

She had called her mother in San Diego and talked with her brother, who would pass it on to mom and she could tell he was worried she was going to ask that they come be with her. Instead, she said, all that distance, what was the use? There was nothing they could do for Orion now. Her mother had been glad to get out of the house, the way Orion took over, making one of the bedrooms his study and stacking all those records of Younger Real Estate all over the room. Once he found those, he never mentioned his dissertation again. When Marcia asked about it he growled that he was doing research, what did she think? What all those old papers had to do with anything, she didn't know. But they were what got him started on the poor Indians. He remembered to call them Native Americans with others, but when he spoke to her they were Injuns.

Already Orion seemed a stranger, someone she had hardly known. What a change from before their marriage to after. Not that it seemed much of a wedding, with a judge in the courthouse. It had been over in five minutes. When they went through the revolving doors onto Main Street she had thought those five minutes weren't much different from the five minutes before and after. They had gone to a motel by the toll road and then to Niles for a couple days and it had been everything she had dreamed, more or less. She could believe that a great change in her life had occurred, and nothing would be as it had been. Maybe she would quit working at the Huddle.

"Don't do that. Not yet."

"Your stipend is enough for the two of us. We won't have to pay rent." And until her mother left, they had lived off her. Her mother had always done the shopping. Orion went sometimes, but her mother had expected him to chip in and he didn't. Where would they have been if she hadn't kept on at the Huddle after Orion had been dropped from the graduate program?

Scott came back after the police left, just letting himself in with the key she had given him. She didn't want him standing outside,

203

waiting for her to open the door. But if anyone noticed him just coming and going with
his own key it would look worse. Well, she
didn't care. Only a few of the people who had
lived here when she was growing up remained. The university had bought up a few
houses and torn them down. That's why there
was the big lot in back that the man facing Ivy
Road rented on game weekends.

"I have to go to the funeral parlor."

"I better not go with you there."

"Well, I don't want to go alone."

"Call Carlotta. The Bacons will go with
you."

Why didn't she resent his deciding things
the way she had Orion's? Scott had been so
sweet. She might have thought he was taking
advantage, her being bereaved and all, but he
seemed only to want to comfort her.

Russell Bacon drove her to the funeral
home on Cleveland Avenue and the traffic
was getting heavy, people going home, but
football fans arriving too. Marcia had never
been to a funeral home before. She had been
too young when her father died. It had been
some time before she realized that he would
never be coming home again. All she remembered of him was his cough, he was always coughing, and then the coughing
stopped and he wasn't there anymore. Why

couldn't it be that way now?

She didn't recognize Orion. They explained to her that the suit had been bought for the occasion — she had told them when they phoned that Orion didn't own a suit — and it gave him a strangely grown-up look. His face looked waxy and unreal.

"You were members of Sacred Heart?"

"Orion was, I guess. I'm not Catholic."

"Father Gerald will say the rosary Sunday night. Monday seemed best for the funeral, because of the game."

They left her alone with the body, closing the doors of the viewing room, and Marcia retreated to the side of the room, but she couldn't get out of sight of that waxen face. Finally she went up to him and talked, telling him what had been going on, everyone had been so nice. She didn't mention Scott, of course.

When she opened the doors and looked out, Carlotta was sitting in a plush red chair crying.

"What's the matter?"

Carlotta looked up at her with tear-filled eyes, and then she stood and took her in her arms, and they rocked back and forth. For the first time, Marcia wept.

30

Schippers flew in for the game, just letting Miss Trafficant know he was coming in his private plane.

"I'll be picking up several others on the way. We will be five in all."

"Did you want to go to the game?"

"Of course."

That was a problem, but tickets could be commandeered from members of the Congregation. Several hours later, Schippers walked in with his party, all of them, like himself, trustees. They wore similar grim expressions.

"Is he expecting us?"

The chancellor had summoned his advisors when Anita told him of Schippers's call, and they had been in there behind closed doors ever since. The president and provost, too. Ballast had popped out now and again.

"Coffee," he had said the first time, and went back inside.

She served them coffee. Silence fell over the gathering while she was in the office, but she heard them start up again as she closed the door. Big powwow.

"You got any AA batteries?" Ballast asked the next time he popped like a cuckoo out of the chancellor's office. His Palm Pilot had gone dead. "I'll bring them in," she said, having had an inspiration.

She called Harold and asked him to bring her some AA batteries.

"It'll be a while."

"You running out of energy?"

"Not likely."

"They're for the chancellor. Emergency."

He dropped whatever he was doing and came. He had picked up the batteries at the bookstore.

"I thought you had those things in stock."

"Why would we?"

"Wait. I'll be right back."

She tapped and entered, and silence seemed to go like a wave before her. Ballast took the batteries and looked apologetically at the others, but he was ignored. She closed the door again on the resumed discussion.

Harold was not in the office. She couldn't believe it. She had called up his personnel file and wanted to show it to him and ask about his middle name. It was right there on the screen. She had half expected to find him looking at it when she returned.

She sat, but her spirits sank lower than she

did. What an unpredictable guy he was beginning to be. She tapped a key and the file came up. She leaned forward, her mouth open. Harold's middle name had disappeared from the first line of his personnel file.

Her buzzer sounded and she went into the chancellor's office. He looked worse than he had when he came back from being kidnapped. The trustees were in a ring facing the desk, the chancellor's advisors scattered about the edges of the room.

"Can we accommodate all these gentlemen for the game tomorrow?"

"I called Corby and have four. Finding a fifth won't be difficult."

"Would you get us rooms in the Morris Inn?"

Anita looked at Schippers. The Morris Inn was booked in perpetuity for game weekends. The chancellor controlled three rooms. She explained this.

"We'll double up."

All the other multimillionaires nodded. They seemed to like the prospect of roughing it.

"Of course you're my guests," the chancellor said.

They had never doubted that by the looks they exchanged.

"Maybe we should continue this without kibitzers, Father."

Schippers said this to the president, refer-ring to the chancellor's advisors. Father Bloom seemed about to protest, but Ballast had risen and then the others followed suit. Anita held the door for them. The chancellor watched them go as if he were being aban-doned.

Ballast said, "They'll eat him alive."

"What's he done?"

"You heard him. He didn't know how to reassure them that everything is all right."

"He'll tough it out."

They wandered away, instructing her to call them immediately if the chancellor asked for them.

"Maybe we should wait here."

"I have work to do."

The interruption had served to take her mind off Harold's surprising departure after she had explicitly asked him to stay. Did he find her bossy? She was bossy. Somebody had to be around here.

The local evening paper arrived. Not the *Picayune*, which in any case had decided to lay off the university, but the other one. They had decided to fill the vacuum created by the *Picayune*'s failure to follow up its scoop. The story was on the front page, running along the bot-tom third of the page. It told of the mysterious death of Orion Plant, who had been researching the legitimacy of the transfer of the land the university stood on. The clear implication was that these events were connected. There was no mention of the chancellor's having been kidnapped. Orion's summary dismissal from the graduate school was mentioned with the heavy implication that this had been a species of retaliation.

Feeling devilish, Anita made copies of the story and took them in to the chancellor and his guests.

31

Roger surrendered his ticket so Phil could take Lieutenant Stewart to the game. The two attended the pep rally Friday night as well, but Roger did not repine. He was able to keep his appetite for athletics under control and had been to many more games than he had really wanted in order to keep Phil company. After all, Notre Dame athletics had been the decisive point in Phil's agreeing to move to South Bend when Roger received his unexpected but welcome offer of the Huneker Chair of Catholic Studies. He invited Whelan from the archives to a spaghetti dinner, with wine for Whelan and a huge tossed salad for them both. The associate archivist was delighted. His infernal stammer mysteriously disappeared when he was with Roger Knight, as long as there were no other people around.

"I'll bring what I've found."

"That is not why I'm asking you."

"I'll have it in my brief case anyway."

"I've brought *The Book of Kills*," he said when he was settled in a chair with a preprandial glass of wine.

This was the document that had been put together by an amateur researcher who was much in the archives, a list of all the mysterious deaths that had occurred on or near the campus over the years.

"Had she found out about Cruelle, the murderer of Indians?"

"I've added that. Information was scattered about."

It was all Roger could do not to start in on the document immediately, but his duties as a host came first. He added the spaghetti to the boiling water, put in a dash of salt, and gave an unnecessary stir to the salad. Shortly the pasta was al dente and they settled down to eat. Whelan was on his third glass of Chianti when Roger cleared the table, anxious to study *The Book of Kills*. But his interest was in the new material Whelan had gathered on the murder of Indians, half a dozen over a year's time, a quarter century after the founding of the university.

After some minutes Roger looked at Whelan, who was refilling his glass. "Are there descendants of Cruelle still about?"

"Not by that name," Whelan said with a fluency unusual even when he was with Roger. "I am still in the process of tracking them down."

"If you find any, they are not likely to be happy that all that sad history of the family has been paraded in the newspapers."

"There was another tonight." Whelan fished the newspaper from his brief case.

"They all but accuse the university of assassinating Orion Plant," Roger said as he perused the piece.

"In that I am sure they are wrong."

"Of course. But a veiled accusation can do more harm than an unequivocal one."

"It is a chilling thought that there is a murderer at large."

Whelan used the phrase with the ease of one who claimed to read a thriller every other day. What did he read on the off days? The Western Canon. They had discussed the attacks on the great works of literature rampant now in the English departments of the nation, with inroads of leveling made even locally. Whelan scoffed at classes offered in mystery fiction.

"It is of course possible for a thriller to be more than a thriller. I could give you instances."

"This is an area where I am completely out of the picture."

"But even if such a book rose to the level of literature, the genre is far down on the spectrum. It is nonsense to suggest otherwise."

"Once all current fiction and poetry were absent from curricula. I suppose the idea was that these could be read on one's own while the verdict on them was slowly formed."

Whelan was *in medio iubilationis* when he left, and Phil had not yet returned. Audible from the campus were the rumblings of the gathering crowd, anxious for the morrow's game. The night air was cold when he saw Whelan off. He watched his friend depart with carefully measured steps, walking becoming in his condition a deliberate act requiring all his attention. Roger looked up at the clear sky and Whelan's phrase came back to him. A murderer at large. And so there was, and doubtless he was more afraid than anyone who thought of him.

32

Quinlan had heard of the unscheduled descent of the most powerful of the trustees, the news coming from Miss Trafficant via Trepani, and the president of the faculty senate was certain he knew the reason for their visit. The series of episodes and revelations had put the administration in a bad light, but now the light was sinister with the discovery of the body of Orion Plant. The wake was scheduled for Sunday night, and Quinlan intended to be there, to show the flag. It would be interesting to see how the administration handled this. Would they try to ignore the tragic death of this young graduate student?

Quinlan was ensconced at a table in the back bar of the University Club, drinking Guinness from bottles. One more sacrilege among so many. This table was his usual haunt on game weekends, and his companions were his regular table mates on such occasions.

"I suppose they put the sudden arrivals in Moreau Seminary."

"No," said Trepani, her teeth exposed.

"They're all in the Morris Inn."

"Who was evicted, I wonder?"

"The adminstration would not have dared give them other than royal treatment."

Quinlan's normal attitude toward trustees was indistinguishable from his attitude toward the administration. He was an ex officio attendant at trustees meetings, without a vote, and from observation he had conceived a deep-seated dislike for the officious Schippers. The multimillionaire had taken on a proprietary air toward the university as his contributions multiplied. It was irksome that Schippers was a collector of rare books and spoke of them as if they were more than commodities, collectibles. But it was a characteristic of trustees that they sought to mimic professional scholars, working up little bits of learned lore to parade at their gatherings. But the enemy of my enemy is my friend.

Quinlan's conception of a university was medieval, a corporation made up of professors, some of whom did administrative duty on short terms to facilitate the essential work. Now there was a professional class of administrators who pretended to an expertise that was independent of any involvement in the teaching and learning that took place on campus. Worse, these parasites behaved as if the faculty were their employees. Public relations people spoke for the university, rehearsed by others who were strangers to the classroom. And there was an infrastructure as well, a pullulating mob who more or less autonomously made decisions that by rights should be made by the faculty. It grieved him to think that students received more direction from these anonymous men and women than they did from the faculty. What image must alumni carry away from the place?

Heidi Aufklarung, a deconstructionist from the English department and a regular at the Quinlan table, had drunk deep and was now repeating the lecture she had given that afternoon. Quinlan tuned her out. It was difficult to champion the faculty when they were before one's eyes. Sandra Trepani was raking her lower lip with her upper teeth and swiveling her glass of mineral water mindlessly. Heidi's voice rose as she made a particularly nihilistic point. Raul Calderon and Jacques Nadir were poised to pose difficulties when Heidi paused for breath.

In the club beyond, the level of noise rose as people came in from the pep rally. Two tall men looked in, saw that all the tables were occupied, and stood at the bar. Trepani leaned toward Quinlan.

"The one on the left is the brother of Roger Knight."

"Don't tell me he is on the faculty too."

"He's a detective."

Ah. The administration's man, hired to harass Orion Plant. On another occasion Leif Quinlan might have brooded over the anomalous way in which Roger Knight had been hired. As a university professor he had not come directly under any department's appointment and tenure committee, though his name had been passed through several in a pro forma way. It did not help that Roger Knight, without any previous teaching experience, had proved to be a popular and innovative teacher. Quinlan had actually toyed with the idea of sitting in on the seminar Knight had offered on Barbey d'Aurevilly, but had thought better of it. He might have seemed to be spying on a colleague. Roger had listened with wide unblinking eyes when Quinlan explained to him the crucial importance of the faculty senate.

"Do you have power?"

"Largely moral."

"The best kind."

Why did he feel that the massive Huneker Professor found him amusing? Quinlan heaved himself to his feet and suddenly felt the impact of the alcohol he had consumed. He stood for a moment, hoping for his head to clear, and then moved to the bar.

"I am Professor Quinlan. I understand you are the brother of Roger Knight."

"I am Philip Knight," the other man said. "You are also speaking to Lieutenant Stewart."

"Lieutenant?"

"South Bend Police."

"Aha. On duty, I presume."

"We've been to the pep rally."

"Good God."

"You don't go?"

Quinlan let his eyes roll upward and then wished he hadn't; it had made him dizzy. "Are you investigating our murder?"

"Did you know the victim?"

"Only indirectly. Only indirectly." Trepani joined them, smiling toothily. Quinlan reluctantly introduced her. "You would do well to speak with Professor Ranke."

"His daughter once went with Orion," Sandra said confidingly. "Before he married."

"She seems to have disappeared."

"What?" Stewart had a way of looking at his interlocutor with great concentration, and Quinlan's reaction was as much an effort to deflect that gaze as to express surprise, though he was indeed surprised. As was Trepani.

"Oh, I hope nothing has happened to her too!"

"The campus should be swept," Quinlan said. "God knows what would turn up."

"Professor Quinlan is president of the faculty senate," Sandra said.

"I thought I recognized your name," Philip Knight said, and now his look too was searching. What on earth had his brother told him?

"We are officially very concerned about recent events on campus. As well as startling revelations that have appeared in the public press. And now a murder. May I ask how your investigation is proceeding?" Quinlan said this archly, mindful that the two detectives had been wasting the evening at the pep rally.

"In a routine fashion," Stewart said in a tone that did not encourage further inquiry.

"Can I buy you a drink?" Philip Knight asked.

It was an indication of Quinlan's discomfort that he refused. "I must get back to my friends. I only wanted to greet you."

He bumped into a chair during his return journey, but did not lose his balance. He regained his chair without incident and Sandra slipped into hers.

"Pompous bastards," Quinlan said in a carrying voice.

"I will bet that Laverne Ranke is lying dead somewhere on this campus at this very minute."

"Very likely. Very likely. While the constabulary disports itself at the bar."

Quinlan picked up his glass and drank deep.

33

The foul weather of the preceding week lifted as if dragged away from the campus and stadium by one of the little planes hired to tow banners overhead for the edification of spectators before heading out of sight taking their messages with them. Thus, the rain and wind and cold seemed taken away to reveal a blue sky, cottony puffs of cloud and sunshine.

Jimmy was waiting for Phil at the designated spot a full fifteen minutes ahead of time, proving that his enthusiasm for the game was not feigned.

"I haven't been to one of these since I was a kid and we used to sneak in."

"Was that possible?"

"Possible but rare."

They toured the campus, enjoying hot dogs and hamburgers and various other burnt offerings sold by the different residence halls or student organizations in order to raise money for some good cause. Smoke rose from the makeshift grills and the delicious smell of health-threatening foods filled the air. The band was ending its concert when they arrived at Bond Hall, and when the players formed up to march to the stadium, Phil and Stewart fell in behind along with thousands of others. It was impossible not to walk to the beat of the band.

Before they went inside, they resupplied with popcorn and massive soft drinks in a container suitable for keeping. Phil's seats — his and Rogers — were in the southwest curve of the stadium. Taking their seats as point B and extending from it two legs of a right angle gave one the south goal posts as the terminus of BA while BC pointed to the right of the north goal posts. The perspective on the game was, Phil felt, ideal. From the end zones it was difficult to calculate the yardage won or lost by a play and from the fifty yard line, where the chancellor's party was ensconced, save for the rare occasions when the teams were at midfield, one had an imperfect view of what went on to the right or left.

"So you picked out these seats with all that in mind?"

Phil smiled. "No, Jimmy. They were issued at random."

Today's game between Indiana and the Irish was a novelty, an addition to the schedule in a year when Purdue had unbreakable commitments elsewhere. Of course, games were arranged years in advance and this contest had been greeted with dismay or jocularity when it was first announced, but in the interval Indiana had gradually built the best team in its history. They were tied with Michigan for the lead in the Big Ten and were scheduled to meet their rival for that position the following week. It was the local hope that, in the phrase, Indiana would be looking beyond this game to the great contest that lay ahead of them. Equally rare, the fans seemed equally divided between the two teams, although there were many with divided loyalties. Everyone was prepared for a historic game.

When Indiana took the field, their band struck up, almost drowning out the good-natured derision of Irish fans. And then, after dramatic hesitation in the mouth of the tunnel leading from the locker rooms, the Irish became visible and the just-returned students, who by tradition stood throughout the game, began to cheer. And then the players ran onto the field, led by the cheerleaders, enveloping the coaching staff. The Fighting Irish had long been a misnomer for the team: African-Americans were a majority and the plucky little quarterback, though named Doyle, was a Eurasian. Father Riehle, the team chaplain, on his gimpy legs, trailed the team in a semblance of jogging. Once settled on the sidelines, the teams sent their captains to the center of the field for the coin toss, which Notre

Dame lost. Indiana elected to receive and then a hush fell over the stadium for the singing of "America the Beautiful" and, to the raising of the flag, the "Star Spangled Banner." With Old Glory rippling nicely in a slight breeze, the teams arranged themselves for the initial kick and the tension and noise mounted.

The Irish kicker advanced on the teed-up ball, toe met pigskin, and the ball soared toward the Indiana goal. It was caught in the end zone. Prudence might have dictated grounding the ball and beginning on the twenty, but after the slightest pause the Indiana special team formed in front of the ball carrier and began the run. The Notre Dame team converging on them were knocked aside like ten pins, and the runner was almost in the clear with nothing between him and the far goal but the Notre Dame kicker. What looked like a perfect tackle proved not to be, the runner lifted one leg free and then the other and was on his way to a touchdown. With less than a minute played, Indiana led 7–0. Notre Dame received, downed the ball in the end zone, and began on its own twenty. Three plays later, they were on their own fifteen, and had to punt. Indiana received the ball on their own twenty-five and advanced it to the middle of the field. Minutes later, they kicked a field goal, bringing the score to 10–0.

The opening provided an omen for the first half. Doyle's passes were inaccurate or dropped, the Irish running game could not be established, Indiana led 24–0 when the teams left the field at half time. The Irish fans around Phil and Stewart had groaned and complained and finally voices were heard in open criticism of coaches and team. Frailty, thy name is football fan. Fair weather loyalists turned on their team when the fortunes of the game went against them. But the true fan waited in the hope that the second half would differ from the first. And so it did. But in the meantime, there was apprehension in the chancellor's box and in the presidential party lest the interruption of the week before be repeated. It was not.

Notre Dame received at the beginning of the second half, the runner taking the ball to the thirty yard line. From there, the Irish marched down the field, mixing passes and runs, and when they were stopped, successfully kicked a field goal. 24–3. The disappearance of that 0 from the scoreboard was a harbinger of things to come. Indiana took possession of the ball, their first play was a pass, and it was gathered in nicely but by an Irish player who scampered toward the goal line with the whole stadium on its feet. When the band's all but constant rendition of the

Notre Dame fight song became audible again, the score was 24–10. An Indiana runaway was turning into a contest.

As if to prove the interception a fluke, the Indiana quarterback connected with his tight end, who advanced the ball to the Notre Dame forty yard line. Minutes later, Indiana was at the Notre Dame four with a first down, four tries to punch the ball across for a touchdown. But for three plays, the Notre Dame defense held, and when Indiana tried a field goal, a Notre Dame defender leapt high in the air and deflected the ball. Notre Dame took over on its own twenty.

The genuine Notre Dame fan is able to recall with apparent accuracy every play in every game he witnessed and of many others besides. The Indiana-Notre Dame game played that Saturday afternoon under a clear sky and comfortable temperatures would enter the annals as one of the top dozen or so games in the history of the school. It was certainly the most exciting and memorable game of the new millennium.

With five minutes to play, the score stood at 27–27. The first teams were weary, but this was no game for substitutions. Doyle had won back the cheers of those who had demanded his removal in the first half. Jefferson had gained more yards running than ever before in his distinguished career and the wide receiver, Toyanga, had gathered in three touchdown passes. As the game approached its end, fans of both teams had ample reason for pride. No matter who won now, both teams had played a game to be remembered. In the event, Indiana won by two points, a safety when Doyle, dodging around desperately in his own end zone, looking for a receiver, could not get a pass off before he was smothered by three Indiana defenders.

29–27. It was a loss, but it had not been a defeat. The Irish, holding their golden helmets high, took the cheers of the student body and then left the field. Phil and Stewart remained for the postgame appearance of the Irish band.

The seats around them emptied, fans going at a snail's pace down the steps to the exits. When the two men stood, Jimmy, looking out at the field, spoke.

"We've had a bit of luck. Anyway, I guess it's luck."

"What's that?"

"The tire track at the scene where Plant's body was found? We've identified it."

"A university vehicle?"

Jimmy turned to him. "Sort of. Phil, the imprint matches the tire on your brother's golf cart."

34

The astonishing identification of the tire imprint near the dead body of Orion Plant required that Roger establish his whereabouts at the time Orion was killed, something easily done though it brought with it the unease of such a need. What if he had been unable to prove that he had been elsewhere with unimpeachable witnesses?

"Of course," Jimmy said, "it wasn't that we really suspected you. But examination of the cart indicates that it was used to transport the body."

The cart had been taken away for this examination and was still in the custody of the police.

"You don't chain it up or anything?"

"Without the key, how could anyone start it?"

But the key was in the ignition when the technicians who had been examining all likely vehicles and were about to give up the search as fruitless noticed Roger's cart parked in a space before the building that housed the Knight apartment. The examination had begun as a final pro forma fillip but had turned into the long-sought golden slipper. With Jimmy, Phil and Roger, about to set off for Orion Plant's funeral in Sacred Heart, began to discuss the puzzling problem of who could have gotten hold of Roger's key, who would have made use of the golf cart for such a gruesome purpose. They had made no progress when it was time to leave for the basilica.

The president said the Mass, assisted by the chancellor and a vice-president. The sanctuary was packed with members of the Congregation. Marcia Plant would have been alone in the pew reserved for mourners had not Carlotta Bacon joined her there. In the front pew on the opposite side of the aisle were the trustees who had been flown in by Schippers on Friday and had remained with him after a series of unsatisfying conferences with the administration. The upshot of their meetings was the strong suggestion that the university not rely on the forgetfulness that time might bring but to prepare and issue a detailed White Paper that would spell out the events that had preceded Father Sorin in this place and the way in which he had gotten title to the land. The university's own treatment of Native Americans was to be highlighted, among them the inclusion of Indians as students from the first. The idea was not simply to answer questions and accusations but to swamp them with a full picture of the university's record on matters that had recently come to the fore.

Orion Plant lay in his casket in the middle aisle where it had been wheeled by the six students acting as pall bearers. The casket was covered with a white silk cloth. Thus, honored and blessed and being sent on his way into eternity lay the man who had been at the origin of recent troubles on the campus. Stewart's cohorts had discovered incontrovertible evidence that Orion had been involved in the kidnapping and were trying to find out who his fellow felons had been. Roger wondered if perhaps some of them were among the pall bearers. He had identified Bacon and Byers and Wilson, another student of Otto Ranke's. All of them were resident in graduate student housing and would have known of Roger's golf cart.

The Mass proceeded with great solemnity, not a requiem Mass as it would once have been, with the vestments black and a black cover over the catafalque and the dirgelike refrains of the *Dies Irae* reminding the living of the dire day that lay ahead when they must answer for their deeds before one who could neither deceive nor be deceived. The new liturgy had a way of suggesting that any and all of the departed were transported swiftly to heavenly bliss. The doctrine of purgatory was not so much denied as ignored, and as for hell, well, this did not seem the time to introduce so sobering a topic.

The homily was preached by Gumble, a young priest who served as chaplain in married student housing and was a marvel of generic praise of graduate students that seemed only tangentially related to the life of Orion Plant. When the Mass was done, two speakers mounted the pulpit and reminisced about the deceased. Russell Bacon was first and was followed by Professor Otto Ranke. Bacon directed his remarks to Marcia and soon had both her and Carlotta weeping uncontrollably. Otto Ranke extolled the life of scholarship, the lure of research, and spoke of the deceased Orion's passion in the pursuit of the past. That he had been cut off so young in his endeavors was a loss to them all, to the university and to the profession. Of course nothing was said of the fact that Orion had been dismissed from the graduate program.

Orion was buried in Cedar Grove, the cemetery where he had desecrated the graves, or had been responsible for their desecration. It had proved easier to link him with the kidnapping than with that outrage. When the body was lowered into the earth on what had once been the sixteenth fairway of the old golf course, Marcia once more broke into tears, her weeping rivaled by that of Carlotta Bacon. The two women clung together as the party dispersed.

A luncheon in the University Club was hosted by the faculty senate but not attended by the administration or trustees. They had gone their extra mile and were not disposed to add to it. Roger and Phil, accompanied by Stewart, whose professional interest in all this was constant but indiscernible, went on to the University Club where they were greeted by Quinlan.

"I didn't think they would dare show their faces here," he said, feeling no need to identify the administration as the object of his scorn.

"He received the full treatment," Roger replied as Phil and Stewart escaped from this male Cassandra. The bar was open and promised surer solace.

"What else could they do? It was an exercise in hypocrisy."

"The tribute that virtue pays to vice."

"You can say that again," Quinlan growled, apparently not catching the inversion of the adage. "I wonder if the police will conduct a genuine investigation and find out who killed the poor devil."

A very genuine investigation was conducted in subsequent days, with the surprising result that Russell Bacon was taken in for questioning and eventually charged with the murder of Orion Plant.

35

Lieutenant Stuart's crew had successfully pursued the one firm clue they had, the tire imprint at the place where the body had been discovered by Father James while feeding the ducks and communing with them in what he presumed was their language, inspired by Saint Francis of Assisi. Matching or trying to match the imprint with university vehicles that had tires of the required dimensions had led nowhere until someone noticed Roger Knight's golf cart and the identification was made. But if Roger's cart was the vehicle in which the body of Orion Plant had been carried to the spot where it was found, new lines of investigation were opened.

Since the cart had been parked by Roger in a space in front of the building where he and Phil lived, and since Roger had not used it on the fatal night and had indeed been provably elsewhere, the question arose as to who had used it. Whoever had used it needed the ignition key to start the motor. Although Roger had at first thought he had taken the key from the ignition after his last use of the cart, further reflection introduced the worm of doubt. It was possible that he had not removed the key. Often in the past he had forgotten to do so. That meant that the cart had been there for the taking. But this led on to several presuppositions.

• It was likely that the one who had employed it for the grisly purpose of moving Orion Plant's body had prior knowledge of the cart. While this did not limit the person to graduate student housing, those who lived there certainly had noticed the gargantuan Huneker Professor of Catholic Studies coming and going in what he had made look like a miniature car.

• While Orion Plant and his wife, Marcia, had not lived in the graduate student village, their home was not fifty yards to the east on Bulla Road.

• After the disappearance of Orion, there was frequent traffic back and forth between the village and the Plant residence. This had taken on a new significance after Stewart talked with Professor Ranke.

Ranke had preferred being interviewed in his home rather than his campus office, and

Stewart was happy to oblige. He refused an offer of schnapps but gladly accepted a cup of coffee.

"Would you prefer tea?" Mrs. Ranke asked. The professor's wife was transformed from the distraught *hausfrau* Stewart had met earlier.

"Coffee, please."

"Despite her Bavarian origins, Freda has become a devotee of tea." It sounded like a line from Gilbert and Sullivan.

When the coffee had been served and he was left alone with Ranke, Stewart said, "You realize, Professor, that I am investigating the death of Orion Plant."

"The murder of Orion Plant."

"Precisely. I would appreciate hearing anything you think might be helpful."

"Of course."

"Who would have had reason to kill the young man?"

"Am I a suspect?" Ranke asked with a puckish smile.

"Not at present," Stewart said with a chuckle. "Did he have enemies?"

The response was extended, beginning with a sketch of Orion's career since he was admitted to the graduate program in history at Notre Dame. Ranke described him as a young man with intelligence, not of the highest, but more than sufficient to complete the program successfully. However, things had conspired to prevent this.

"He married, but that is sometimes a spur to swifter completion. That was not so with Orion. He dithered. Not because he was lazy but because his interests diverged from the topic of his dissertation."

"Native Americans."

"Yes. I warned him, scolded him, cajoled him. As his dissertation director, I defended him when his case came up for review before the graduate committee, an annual event. But the time came when I too gave up on him."

"Plagiarism?"

"How odd that you should mention that."

Stewart had mentioned it because of something Roger Knight had said, and then the story came of Bacon's presenting as his own a paper that Orion had read to Ranke's seminar some years before.

"Was he formally accused?"

Ranke nodded. "I am a member of the college ethics committee that heard the case."

"And?"

"He was exonerated."

"So he was falsely accused?"

"No. He was guilty as charged. But the incriminating evidence had been destroyed."

"How did you notice that his paper was really Plant's?"

"Orion noticed it. It was on top of a pile of papers on my desk. We were talking, the phone rang, and while I was occupied his eye dropped to the paper. Soon he was reading it avidly. When I finished with the phone, he told me the paper was identical with his own. I quickly dispelled the notion that I had kept his original paper there. In any case, this one bore Bacon's name as author. Orion subsequently proved to me beyond a doubt that the papers were not only identical but that his text had been downloaded from his computer."

"That was the evidence that was destroyed?"

"The file was erased from Orion's hard drive. The case evaporated."

"Did Bacon know that Orion was his accuser?"

"Yes."

It was not an accusation that one would take lightly, particularly if he were guilty. Ranke might have had to rely on what Orion put before him, but Plant had first-hand certainty that Bacon had stolen his seminar paper and submitted it as his own. Had Bacon seen Orion Plant as an albatross around his neck, the perpetual possibility that in years to come his plagiarism would accompany his career if only as a rumor?

The interview went on, but nothing else was relevant to Stewart's inquiry.

"Has your daughter come home?"

"Yes, thank God."

As he left, Stewart had a fleeting glimpse of a young woman peering at him from another room and quickly withdrawing when their eyes met.

Before talking with young Bacon, Stewart brought the lab boys — two of them women — back to campus where they inspected the area around the parking space of Roger's vehicle. There were footprints galore, of course, but several particularly deep ones caught their attention. They made impressions. A match was made with a pair of Bacon's shoes. A crucial moment had arrived: That Bacon could be shown to have been near Roger's vehicle, that the imprint of his shoes was deep even though snow had been falling — perhaps the snow served to preserve them — suggesting he had been carrying something heavy, this was the most circumstantial of evidence. That a resident of the village should leave footprints all about the place was hardly incriminating. Bacon had visited Roger Knight within the week of the murder. But when Stewart explained to Bacon what they had found, his wife Carlotta let out a shriek. Unnerved, Bacon blurted out his story. Yes, he had used Roger Knight's golf cart to remove the body of Orion Plant.

"But it's not what you think! I didn't kill him."

He was taken downtown and booked. Bartholomew Leone offered his services pro bono and appeared with his new client at the arraignment. But not even the mellifluous Leone could get Bacon free on bail. The young man languished in the county jail, awaiting trial, insisting that he had not killed Orion Plant. He had found the body and carted it away. Perhaps Leone believed this, but Stewart had long experience with accused killers. Bacon could scarcely deny the evidence that had been amassed. But despite his admission he clung to the notion that the obvious implication could not be drawn.

Stewart would have been more content with this outcome had not Chief Kocinksi been so unctuous in his praise. Moreover, he received a call of congratulation from Ballast, the university counsel. If only Bacon would admit to killing Orion Plant.

36

Anita Trafficant was as relieved as anyone in the Main Building when Bacon was arrested. Maybe more so. That the culprit proved to be a graduate student in good standing — although the story of his being accused of plagiarism became known; it was, after all, the presumed motive for what he had done — displeased the chancellor. He would have preferred some total stranger descending on the campus in the midst of a snowstorm and wreaking havoc.

"They wouldn't have caught a total stranger," Anita observed.

"I suppose you're right. To think that fellow was my kidnapper. What had I ever done to him?"

"It wasn't you he kidnapped," Anita said. "He kidnapped the chancellor of Notre Dame."

Like any occupant of office, the chancellor had difficulty distinguishing between his private person and the official position he held. He had come to fuse the two in his mind and looked forward to reappointments into the indefinite future. That desire had been shaken by his ordeal and only recently reasserted itself. The president had a committee at work producing the White Paper the trustees had suggested. Suggested? It had been a condition of their not making a devastating proposal to the full board of trustees. Their determination had been weakened by the exciting game they had seen on Saturday and now the arrest of Bacon altered the picture completely. Like another high official, and with infinitely less cause, he had faced impeachment and removal from office. But now the cloud had gone.

A cloud had lifted in Anita Trafficant's mind as well. The inescapable fact that Harold had altered his personnel file, removing the middle name that suggested a connection with that long-ago slayer of Indians, set off dark suspicions. Had Harold decided to stop the renewed condemnation of his ancestor? Anita had become uncomfortable with Harold and, she felt, he was equally uncomfortable with her. Had she failed to disguise the thoughts she had? But now the killer had been found and once more sun shone on South Bend, on the campus of Notre Dame, and on Anita Trafficant.

"What is your middle name?" she asked Harold.

They were dining in the Lasalle Grill where he had been commenting on the minuscule portion of his entrée. Identifying it as nouvelle cuisine had not altered his disappointment. He was sipping his wine when she asked her question. He set his glass on the table.

"You know what it is."

"Cruelle."

"That's right."

"And you deleted it from your personnel file."

"The name has associations and I didn't want you to be influenced by them." He put his hand on hers. She turned hers over and felt his warm palm on hers. To think that she had imagined Harold's could be the hand of a killer.

"Did you think I would be? Something that happened a century ago?"

"His blood runs in mine."

"And Cain's runs in all of us."

He squeezed her hand and let it go. Later, after the wine and the lifting of misunderstanding between them, she half dreaded, half hoped that he would want to come in when he brought her to her door. But he kissed her chastely on the forehead and that was it.

Inside, disappointment gave way to admiration at his tact and the respect it represented. Now if only he would ask the big question.

She was more than ready to stop working and settle down as a housewife and eventual mother. The supposed equality of women had come down to endless dissatisfying jobs where women could enjoy their terminal inequality with men. There was nowhere to go from where she was. What post higher than that of secretary to the chancellor was open to her? And the chancellor, hitherto so olympian in his eminence, had become unglued by the ordeal of kidnapping. This was understandable enough, but the lingering effects of what he had been through seemed permanent. He had been putty in the hands of the Schippers delegation. Anita, of course, acted as liaison with the committee put together to compose the White Paper. To her surprise, Sandra Trepani, the toothy sociologist who was a prominent figure in the faculty senate, was a member. She clearly saw herself as a surrogate for Quinlan.

"White Paper," she had said before the first meeting of the committee, in a sibilant whisper. "White Wash would be more like it."

Anita looked at her. If she was disenchanted with the administration, she was filled with distaste at such faculty contrariness. A pox on both of them.

"Pox *tibi*," she said to Sandra.

"*Et cum spiritu tuo.*" Followed by a conspir-
atorial giggle. Good Lord.

37

Phil had noticed the presence of Byers when he and Stewart talked with Marcia Plant before the body of her husband was found. For some reason he did not seem then, or later when Marcia had become a bereaved widow, like just another friend paying his respects. Others came and went and he remained and only eventually left. This stayed in his mind, and Bacon's adamant refusal to admit that he had done anything more than transport the body to where it was found increased his curiosity. He visited Bacon.

After only a few days in captivity, Bacon looked like the man in the iron mask. Was it possible that he was equally innocent? He had aged, his unwashed hair fell from his head as if it would uproot itself and leave Bacon bald.

"Care to talk?"

"You're Roger Knight's brother?"

"Yes. Philip Knight."

"A private investigator?"

"That's right."

"Can I hire you? How much do you charge?"

"What's the assignment?"

"Find the bastard who killed Orion."

"Do you have anyone in mind?"

Bacon looked wildly about, then shook his head in despair. "I wish I did. But it's not easy wishing someone else in my place, unless I really knew. I don't."

"Let's just talk it through. You are at the great disadvantage of having a motive."

"That paper? I was exonerated."

"Because you destroyed the evidence."

"Who could prove that?"

"Now that Orion's dead? Probably nobody. Of course, Professor Ranke can give second-hand testimony."

"He wouldn't," Bacon said, apparently not knowing that Ranke already had. "Anyway, would I kill someone for that?"

The guilty almost never admit their guilt. Phil knew this. But something about Bacon gave him pause.

"I want to go over every detail with you. Of course you needn't talk to me."

"Can I be your client? How much do you charge?"

"Look, I am still more or less retained by the university. They are satisfied that no mystery remains. In any case, I shall go on investigating the death of Orion Plant."

"You think I'm innocent?" Bacon's expres-

sion was one of surprised, almost servile grati-
tude.

"Until you're proved guilty."

The elation drained from Bacon's eyes.
"Everyone is."

"Let's start at the beginning."

Phil had Bacon go over the sequence of that
fateful night. He had found the body, he had
remembered Roger's golf cart and to his surprise found the key in the ignition. The vehicle made no noise, running on a rechargeable
battery.

"My big fear was that the battery was low,
that I would run out of power before I got the
body out of there. I considered recharging it
at my place, running an extension out from
the apartment."

"That would have taken time."

"And made Carlotta wonder what I was
doing. I had to be careful not to attract her attention. I was so horrified by what I had
found I didn't want her to know."

"Did you go back to your apartment?"

"Of course."

"Why?"

"To pick up the body. That's why I made
off with your brother's golf cart?"

"But didn't you find the body by the
cart?"

"No. It had been put on our front steps."

"Your front steps?"

"Yes."

"You never mentioned that before."

"What difference does it make?"

Phil had long wondered why the body of Orion Plant had been lying next to Roger's golf cart, as had been his assumption and Stewart's all along.

"Probably none," he said, not wanting to raise Bacon's hope. But this was a potentially critical detail. If what Bacon said was true, and the fact that he had revealed the original location of the body so casually suggested it was, someone had placed the dead body of Orion Plant on the Bacon doorstep. The clear reason for that was to draw suspicion away from the perpetrator and to Bacon. Bacon had indeed come under suspicion, but because he had decided to remove the ghoulish evidence from his doorstep.

That night Phil went for a walk up Bulla Road. The lights were on in Plant's house — or his mother-in-law's, as it happened. Phil continued on to Ironwood and then started back. As he was approaching the house again he saw a figure hurry from a car that had not been parked there when Phil first went by. It was a male and at the door he stood for a moment and then let himself in, obviously with a key. Phil had stopped to observe this, and when he continued it was stealthily. At the house he left the road and went across the risible lawn and along the side of the house to the back. Drapes had been pulled over the front windows, but the kitchen windows were ablaze and unshuttered. Inside, Marcia Plant was being embraced by a man who snuggled his face in her hair. And then he drew back. Scott Byers.

Phil went on home, where Roger was engrossed in his global e-mail correspondence. The impulse to tell his brother what he had learned faded. What after all had he learned? The accused continued to deny that he had killed Orion Plant; he had revealed an element in his alleged discovery of the body that seemed critical but might have been a shrewdly planted point to engage the interest of a private investigator he hoped to hire. Byers? However tasteless it was of him to rush to comfort the widow and step into her slain husband's shoes — and of course reciprocally of Marcia Plant to allow him to do so — it would not be the first time a bereaved widow had posted with such dexterity to incestuous sheets, as Roger might have said. He would harbor what he might have learned awhile.

The following day, Phil stopped by the Huddle where Marcia had worked but from which she was now on indefinite compassionate leave. He took a cup of coffee to a table and noticed that at a nearby table several employees were enjoying their break. After a time all but one, an adenoidal youth, got up and returned to their posts. Phil took his coffee to the table and sat. The adenoidal youth looked up. His name tag said Dave.

"Dave, I'm one of the investigators into the death of Orion Plant." He held out his hand and Dave took it, looking alarmed.

"Geez, what a thing to happen, and on campus."

"Are you a student?"

"Not here. At IVY Tech."

"Worked here long?"

"Since I got out of high school."

Unless Dave was a wholly ungifted scholar that had to be some years ago.

"So you know Marcia Plant."

"I still think of her as Marcia Younger. That was her name when I met her."

"You liked her?"

"Everybody likes Marcia. I tried to take her out, but no go. She was determined to land a Notre Dame student."

"Well, she succeeded."

"Yeah. Twice."

"Oh?"

"She was going pretty hot and heavy with

one, and then suddenly she married the guy she married."

"Threw the first one over?"

"And he didn't like it a bit. Used to get in line to get to Marcia and then hold everybody up while he talked to her. Embarrassing."

"You wouldn't know his name?"

Dave shook his head, not even trying to remember. "He was a grad student in math."

Was he referring to Byers?

Dave looked at his watch and let out a theatrical yelp. "I've got to get back."

"Thanks for talking to me."

"No problem."

He did discuss it with Roger then. As he expected, Roger seized on Bacon's claim that he had found Orion's body on his doorstep, not by Roger's cart.

"I suppose if he had, he would simply have sounded the alarm. A body by my cart wouldn't incriminate him. Have you told this to Stewart?"

"I wanted to run it by you first."

"Why don't we give him a call?"

38

Stewart was not enthralled with the idea that he had the wrong man under indictment for the murder of Orion Plant, but he consoled himself with the thought that, even if this should prove to be the case, Bacon was at the least guilty of disturbing the scene of a crime, transporting a corpse, and doubtless other crimes and misdemeanors that an agile prosecutor might come up with. Not that he thought that prosecution likely if what Phil Knight was suggesting was true. He went out to the Knight apartment with the thought that the hospitality sure to be shown there made the trip eminently worthwhile. And so it proved. Phil brought out a bottle of Bushmills never yet opened.

"What are we drinking to?" he asked, lifting his glass.

"Justice," Roger suggested. He had a glass filled with some noxious diet soda in his hand.

"Can't go wrong with that."

Cheerio, bottoms up, and then the velvety liquid slid over his tongue, awoke his taste buds, and descended his throat to begin its synaptic discombobulation. He warned himself to keep a keen mind, remembering Phil's cryptic message when he called.

"I think I may have found the killer of Orion Plant."

"Has Bacon escaped?"

"Come and talk."

Well here he was, initially lubricated and receptive.

"I think you should have a talk with Scott Byers, Jimmy."

"What about?"

Throughout the ensuing narrative, Stewart tried to retain his skepticism, but this became increasingly hard to do. He confessed, if only to himself, that there were aspects of the technical description of the place where Roger's golf cart had been parked that did not satisfy him. Moreover, the fact that Bacon had freely confessed — after his wife's shriek — to having moved the body contrasted dramatically with his continued insistence that he had not killed Orion Plant. What Phil was suggesting removed some of the anomalies — why had Bacon felt compelled to move a body that was lying several doors away and taken the risk of being seen transporting his grim cargo despite the falling snow that night? It galled Stewart that he had not ascertained where Bacon had found the body. Bacon's confession had not asserted but only implied that he had found the body beside the golf cart, hoisted it aboard, and set off for Saint Mary's Lake. A direct question could have turned up what Bacon had casually revealed to Philip Knight. If indeed it had been casual.

"Of course I thought of that. Later. By the way, I gave him no indication that he had added such a significant detail. I was convinced that he did not realize the importance of it. It was his anxiety to remove the body from his wife's possible discovery of it that motivated him, and that eclipsed all other considerations as he told me."

"Have you talked with Byers again?"

"No, no. That is your task."

Jimmy had been aware of the presence of Byers when they visited Marcia Plant, before and after the discovery of the body of her husband. Phil's description of Byers letting himself into the house with a key, and then the embrace in the kitchen, was consonant with what he had seen. But now to hear that Byers was the repudiated swain when Marcia had abruptly married Orion Plant supplied a motive indeed, and one more intelligible to a jury than an apparently exploded accusation of plagiarism.

"I'll talk to him," Stewart said.

And that was that. Neither of the Knight brothers pressed the matter further. More Bushmill's was poured, and as much drunk, and Roger exceeded his limit and had a second diet soda. Talk turned to the following Saturday's game, to be played far away in historically hostile territory in California.

"Stanford is overrated."

Roger nodded vigorously and began to speak of the fate of the humanities in that hitherto great institution of higher learning. Stewart and Phil listened uncomprehendingly, but Roger's evident passion for the subject kept them silent until he was done.

"That is a pushover league," Phil said.

"I like Washington State."

"Because they lead the league? A big fish in a small pond."

The discussion of sports became impassioned and progressively less coherent, and eventually Roger excused himself and went off to his study. Stewart might have taken that as a signal to go, but Phil insisted he stay, drawing attention to the amount of Bushmill's left. Only a boor would have deserted his host with such a problem.

Later, at home, in the wee hours, Stewart made a chart of the facts or purported facts they knew now.

Tuesday. Early evening. A meeting at the Plant home with his band of malcontents.

Present: Orion, Marcia, Bacon and his wife Carlotta, Byers, Laverne Ranke, and several nonstudent members. The general meeting ended and Orion remained with his inner council, Marcia, Byers, and Bacon. Then was hatched the plan to be executed by Orion Plant solo. Dressed in the garb of an Indian, he was to have descended on the grotto and dispersed the group gathered there to say the rosary. The idea was that he was taking possession of ancestral lands. The dispersal of those gathered to pray was considered of great newsworthy potential.

Byers and Bacon and the others left. Orion, in warrior attire, bade his wife a tender good-bye — Marcia had insisted on this, thus implying that such demonstrations of affection were the exception to the rule. Then he had left her, never more to be seen alive by her. He did not return that night and Byers vouched for the fact that Marcia had told him so before the discovery of the body. He had agreed with her decision not to report her husband's absence. Marcia's manner turned icy when she was pressed as to where she thought he might have been that night.

Orion Plant had gotten as far as graduate student housing. Hitherto it had been assumed that he had been attacked near Roger Knight's golf cart. Had it been his intention to use it to get to the grotto? If Bacon was to be believed, he had been attacked and killed on the Bacon doorstep. Why would he have gone there? Bacon's eagerness to get rid of the body when he allegedly discovered it could be explained by his fear of being implicated in the events that Orion had been engineering. Or, of course, for whatever reason, Orion had come to his door, Bacon had gone outside, wrested the tomahawk from the ersatz Indian, and dispatched him to the happy hunting grounds. In either case, he had gone for Roger's cart, got the body aboard, and set off for Saint Mary's Lake, where he unloaded it in the snow below Fatima Retreat House.

Wednesday. Father James, retreat director at Fatima though not the superior of the house, had come upon the body while feeding the ducks on a snowy morning. When he discovered the body, he turned in the alarm. The rest was a matter of police record. The tire print at the scene, after laborious investigation, proved to have been made by a tire on Roger Knight's golf cart, his means of transportation about the campus.

Friday. Bacon, when questioned along with others in the neighborhood of the cart, suddenly blurted out his story. Despite the partial nature of his confession, he was indicted and arraigned for trial on a charge of first-degree murder.

Saturday. Indiana beat Notre Dame in a hotly contested struggle by the score of 29 to 27.

These notes were made in Stewart's head, which admittedly was befogged by substantial amounts of Irish whisky. But, drunk or sober, he was resolved to confront Scott Byers with what had come to light about him and Marcia Plant, née Younger.

39

In unguarded moments, the mind of Otto Ranke was assailed by quotations from Hegel and Goethe, indelibly imprinted on it in his youth. There had been a dangerous period when he had thought alternately of devoting himself to philosophy or to poetry. But his gift lay elsewhere, in the careful reconstruction of the past, allowing no bias or predisposition to color the facts, making his reader an eyewitness of what had happened before either of them had been born. European history had been his focus when he was hired by Notre Dame, but a few years on campus had brought about a fascination with the place where he was living out his professional career. He bought a home close to campus in an area where, at the time, faculty predominated. Now he was the lone survivor. But he, like his late colleagues, had craved proximity to Notre Dame. This was not just another university, a way station on a career that might soon take one elsewhere to a supposedly more prestigious post. By the time he received tenure, Otto Ranke was as confirmed in his love for Notre Dame as the most fanatic alumnus.

His research began to focus on the past of the place. His book on famous authors who had visited Notre Dame had been a work of love and, surprisingly, had enjoyed both critical and popular esteem. He had never equaled it, but the tenor of his research and writing and teaching had been set. An all-male institution when he arrived, Notre Dame had become coeducational in the seventies and Otto Ranke had rejoiced, intending that his only child, Laverne, should attend his university. She balked. It was the first show of the antic opposition that would characterize her future dealings with both her parents. He had lavished affection and cultural advantages on his daughter and she retaliated by espousing the most egalitarian of likes. The immortal strains of Bach and Brahms and Mozart had filled the Ranke house since Laverne was a child. She persisted in listening to orgiastic nonsense, played so loud that the deaf in Mishawaka could have heard it. When she was a child, he had read Stevenson to her, and *The Wind in the Willows*. When she grew older, they read together *The Country of the Pointed Firs* and *My Antonia*. Ostensibly she loved both the music and the literature to which she had been introduced. Ranke could remember with moist eyes discussing the intricacies of Jane Austen's little world with his beloved daughter. Dickens had never taken with her, but she reveled in Trollope. He personally taught her German and was overjoyed to hear her conversing fluently with her mother in the tongue he and Freda had learned as children.

It was her refusal to apply for admission at Notre Dame that marked the turning point. Not even a loving paternal eye could see in Laverne someone young men would find a concupiscible object. All the more reason for her to be inured to higher pleasures.

"It would be like home schooling," she said, when the subject of her going to Notre Dame arose. "I've practically lived on the campus all my life."

He tried reason, he tried threats, Freda resorted to tears. To no avail. A long-lived dream suffered a sudden death.

After this hostility to the university to which Otto Ranke had given his heart and his life, Laverne returned with a library degree and got a job in Hesburgh Library. A menial job. A job he had no wish to tell his colleagues of. It occurred to him that she had taken the job to spite him. But the worst was yet to be. He had introduced an adder into the bosom of his family. Orion Plant came with others from his seminar, but unlike the others he noticed Laverne. A friendship began and prospered. He and Freda made themselves scarce while the young people giggled and laughed in the family room. It had seemed a reasonable hope that marriage was in the offing and that Laverne would end up as a faculty wife, even if not at Notre Dame. And then abruptly, cruelly, offhandedly, Orion informed the professor who had been his solitary champion in the face of more than reasonable complaints that he had married.

Laverne was devastated. Freda was dumbfounded. Otto Ranke was incredulous. Was it possible for a young man so to toy with the affections of a vulnerable female? He restrained himself. He did not tell Orion what he thought of him. He would not give the scoundrel the satisfaction of his paternal indignation at his treatment of Laverne. But he bided his time. When the graduate committee next met, Otto Ranke withheld any defense of his candidate. Orion Plant was justly and rightly dismissed from the program.

The father of children is destined to know dark days that eclipse the bright ones, and there had been no darker day than that on which Otto Ranke again heard the familiar whispering and giggling emerging from his family room. The miscreant was back, the faithless lover had returned, and Laverne, the idiot, had welcomed him.

By then, Laverne had years of practice defying good advice. She seemed to have convinced herself that Orion was as eligible as he ever was because he had married his wife before a judge and had not sought the sanction of the Church. That the incumbent Mrs. Plant might be enraged by such a suggestion did not bother Laverne.

"All's fair in love and war."

Marcia Plant had alienated Orion's affections when Laverne had been sure of them; now, turnabout was fair play. Worse, her renewed relations with Orion had drawn her into his silly plotting to embarrass the university on the matter of its title to its land. He was certain that she had been involved in the atrocity in Cedar Grove, leading Orion into the cemetery by way of the Ranke backyard and returning by the same route. The two of them had been in the family room together, accorded immunity from any inquiry as to what they were up to. They could have done the damage to the cemetery in fifteen minutes. When the toppled tombstones became known, Professor Ranke found incriminating shoes in Laverne's closet and himself removed the telltale clay from them. But he lived in dread that imprints of those soles would be found and an effort made to identify the wearer of those shoes. A demeaning precaution. For all the outrage and disgust that desecration elicited, there had been no serious effort to find the culprits.

The kidnapping of the chancellor was another and far more threatening event. Laverne had left the house in the yellow slicker she had affected, as if she were a homeless person. The garment fairly glowed in the dark. Surely someone would have noticed the wild-eyed young woman wearing it. Ranke took it from Laverne's closet one day when she was arguing with her mother in the kitchen. He drove with it to a Mishawaka mall, removed the balled up Kleenex and other contents from the pockets, tore out the label, and, with the certainty that all eyes were on him when he did so, opened the door of a Dumpster and dropped the slicker inside. The mystery of that missing garment threw the house into disorder; of course, he had not communicated to Freda his fears, but Professor Ranke rode it out in silence. To such lengths will an injured father go to protect his offspring.

With the death of Orion, even darker suspicions grew. Marcia Plant could not have viewed with indifference her husband's inclusion of his once and present love in the conspiring group. He easily imagined the animosity of the two women, rivals for the worthless favor of Orion. Had Laverne been repudiated again? Anyone who learned of these events might suspect that Laverne had availed herself of the obverse of the unwritten law. Once admitted, this thought was difficult to dismiss as incredible. Laverne's prolonged absence from the parental roof would feed the suspicion. Otto Ranke began to fear for his daughter.

The visit of Lieutenant Stewart and Philip Knight had seemed to encircle the question without ever formulating it. Professor Ranke was certain they suspected Laverne. For days he agonized. And then he decided to make the supreme sacrifice.

40

Carlotta Bacon had come to console her at the loss of Orion, and after Russell Bacon had been arrested for the murder the two women became even closer. This was welcome to Marcia, if only because it equalized their conditions, in a sense. Being commiserated with was not something she wanted to get used to. People had a way of treating her as if she were somehow to blame, but she felt they probably meant that Orion had trodden a dangerous path and what had happened to him, while terrible, was not unexpected.

"Why is Scott always hanging around?" Carlotta asked, lifting her brows receptively. There was the slightest playful edge to her voice.

"You'd think he'd wait until the body is cold, wouldn't you?"

"Which body?"

"Carlotta!" But she had laughed, laughed more than the joke deserved, and it was as if she was driving from her system all the rituals of mourning.

"You are eligible again, after all."

"We used to go together once, before I married."

"Aha." But Carlotta looked as if she had already known that.

"We were quite serious. And then Orion came along."

"A historian rather than a mathematician."

"Oh, it wasn't that. Other things aside . . ." she paused and let Carlotta fill in the blank. "Other things aside, Orion was closer to finishing, or so I thought. I wanted to get away from here, not live for years as a student's wife."

"It's not so bad." But a cloud gathered on Carlotta's face. "I tell myself not to worry about Russ. He says he didn't do it and I believe him. I can't imagine him doing harm to anyone."

"No. Still, he didn't hesitate about taking the chancellor into custody." That event had never been called a kidnapping by Orion or any of the others.

Would she have sat talking with Carlotta like this if she thought Russell Bacon had killed Orion? If he had, that wouldn't make Carlotta guilty, anymore than Marcia was guilty of the things Orion had done.

"Laverne Ranke was along on that too."

"Yes."

"I suppose she was a kind of insurance, a

faculty daughter, in case things went wrong. The police wouldn't prosecute a faculty member's child."

"Why not? She's not even a student. Never was."

"You can never get her to really talk about things, you know? She was always aloof at work, and the next thing I know she was recruited by Orion."

Marcia peered at her friend, unable to tell how much knowledge lay behind the remark.

"They used to go together."

"Who?"

"Orion and Laverne Ranke."

"No!"

"Didn't you know that?"

"What happened?"

Marcia smiled. "I stole him away from her."

"And dropped Scott."

"You're sure you never knew about Orion and Laverne?"

"You know, I'm trying to think. I didn't know about it, but now that I do some things make more sense."

"Like what?"

"Like the fact that you two hated each other. I said she was aloof." Carlotta chuckled. "I said to Russ once that Laverne certainly plays her cards close to her chest. He said, she has no choice."

"That's mean." But Laverne *was* straight as a stick. What did men see in women like that? In Orion's case, she suspected it was Laverne's link to his professor.

"Anyway, she took refuge with us for a few days — apparently her father is an absolute tyrant. Russ didn't like it, you know how small the place is, but what could I do? It was like she was asking for sanctuary. Finally Russ told her father. She had a home, it wasn't as if we were throwing her into the street. While she was there we had a chance to talk and she wasn't as close as she usually is." Carlotta paused. "She told me she was in love with Orion."

"Carlotta, she's been carrying a torch ever since Orion and I married."

"When I told her he was married she just looked at me and said, not in my eyes, he isn't."

"The bitch."

She didn't tell Carlotta that Orion had gone back to visiting Laverne, in her parents' house, in the way he had once jokingly told her all about. The professor in his den, the professor's wife knitting in the living room, listening to music, Orion and the daughter being trusted alone in the family room. If she let him in and they spent time in the family

271

room, Orion wouldn't waste time as he claimed he had before he married her. Pathetic, meatless Laverne must have felt like a femme fatale, luring Orion back into her lair. What she wouldn't have done if she learned Orion was just using her. Carlotta was right about that. It was the connection with Professor Ranke that brought Laverne into the group. Orion never spelled it out, but he was setting Laverne up. If she was caught red-handed, it would be his revenge on the professor who had let him down.

"Orion, she'll tell everything she knows."

He had shaken his head, smugly.

"For old times sake?" she'd asked sarcastically.

"She hates her father more than I do."

Scott had been hiding in a bedroom during Carlotta's most recent visit, and Marcia did not hurry the conversation. Let Scott stew up there. He took too much for granted and Marcia worried that she had made things too easy for him. She wished she hadn't given him that key. This morning she had considered taking it from his pocket while he still slept. He would think he'd lost it. And she would take her time about giving him another. Let him worry. It couldn't happen right away, but giving Scott the run of the house might make him less keen to take the trip to the court-house she had made with Orion.

"What were you two talking about?" Scott asked, peeved, when she went up to release him from his hiding place.

"Not you."

"Good."

"What does that mean?"

"Nothing, nothing." He looked tender. "I was thinking of you. Excuse me a minute. I didn't want to use the bathroom while she was here." And he scuttled off in his skivvies. She went to his trousers and took the house key with her downstairs. But she made coffee for him, and scrambled some eggs. When they were seated at the table, a gray day at the window, the game weekend parking lot beyond looking desolate and deserted, she laughed.

"What's funny?"

"She didn't say it right out, but I think Carlotta suspects that you killed Orion so I would be free to marry you."

Scott studied her. "That's desperate. She's trying to protect her husband."

Marcia didn't like the way he danced away from the real purpose of her remark.

"You mean it isn't possible?"

"That I should have killed him?"

"That you should want to marry me."

Suddenly, through the window, she saw Philip Knight looking in at them. He waved. And then the front doorbell rang. Philip Knight had disappeared and Scott had not seen him. He pushed back from the table.

"They know you're here."

"They?"

"The police."

It was Lieutenant Stewart at the front door. Philip Knight came around the house and joined him. "He's inside, Jimmy."

They came in and heard the sound of the back door being unlocked. You wouldn't have thought men that size could move so quickly. They returned with the struggling Scott held securely by his arms.

"We're taking you downtown," Lieutenant Stewart said.

"What for?"

"Why don't we save that for downtown."

Scott looked at her, wild-eyed, and then he calmed down. His expression was now that of a man who has been betrayed.

41

Phil sat in on the interrogation, admiring Jimmy's skills.

"You're entitled to have a lawyer with you."

"What for?"

"We're investigating the death of Orion Plant."

"But you've already arrested Bacon!" He glanced at Phil and then stared at the tabletop. "Carlotta put you up to this, didn't she?"

"Up to what?"

"Oh come on. Look, I didn't kill Orion."

"Why would you deny an accusation that hasn't yet been made?"

"Yet."

"Is there anything you want to tell us?"

"Why don't you tell me why I am here. Maybe I will call a lawyer."

"I'll wait."

Byers's voice had risen in defiance, but now he slumped in his chair.

"We have the murder weapon, you know. The tomahawk. There are prints on it." This was accurate enough except that the prints were smudged beyond recognition.

Byers perked up. "I was wearing gloves that night."

Stewart let the words echo in the room. "Would you like me to get a lawyer for you?"

"I still don't need a lawyer."

"Because you were wearing gloves?"

"That isn't what I meant."

"What did you mean?"

"That I didn't kill anyone."

"Why did you think Carlotta Bacon would accuse you of killing Orion and setting up her husband?"

"Because he's her husband."

"Orion was the husband of Marcia."

"What's that got to do with anything?"

"You've reestablished relations with her, haven't you? Indecently quickly, I might add."

"I've tried to help her through this. We all have."

"But no one else has moved in with the widow."

"I have my own place."

"You have a key to the house. You've been seen letting yourself in as if you owned the place. How many nights would you say you've stayed there?"

There is a rhythm to interrogations. Fear and defiance alternate, anger begins when the same questions are asked again and again. Byers began to have the look of a cornered man. Phil considered the young man's plight.

Jimmy said that they knew Byers had been seeing Marcia right up to her marriage to Orion Plant. "That must have come as a shock to you."

"I was surprised, yes."

"Disappointed?"

"I suppose."

"Angry?"

Byers did not answer. Wondering how anything he said might be taken had made him seem furtive, the manner of someone hiding what the questions were circling toward.

"Damn it, are you going to arrest me or what?"

"On what charge?"

"What you've been hinting at all along."

"What would that be?"

"Come on."

"Why don't you just tell us all about it."

"All about what?"

"What we are talking about."

"That I used to go with Marcia before she got married? That I have been seeing her since Orion was killed? Is that a federal offense?"

"Killing Orion?"

"No. Seeing a woman. Staying with her, so what? She isn't married."

"Because her husband was killed."

"Yes, Orion was killed. That isn't news."

"And that left an open path for you to reclaim your true love."

And so it went. Like Bacon before him, Byers was adamant that he had not killed Orion Plant. Bacon, however, had admitted to removing the body and taking it in Roger's cart and dumping it in the wooded area beneath Fatima Retreat House. The mystery of why he had bothered to do that remained, and it was the hook on which to hang the charge that he had murdered Orion before taking away his body. The case against Byers was more tenuous. He had gone with Marcia and suddenly she had married Orion Plant, leaving him presumably with the standard reaction of the jilted male. He had all but moved in with the new widow after the event, suggesting that this had been the point of killing Orion. But it was all conjecture. Unless, of course, Carlotta Bacon did indeed suspect Byers and had reason for doing so. But would she not then have told the police of her suspicion?

Stewart was off on a tangent, explaining to Byers the procedure for taking him before a judge and making a formal charge. Byers followed this as if it were a technical problem he was glad to be informed of. Finally, Stewart got up.

"I am going to leave you now with Detective Knight. I am going to get a lawyer for you so we can go through all this thoroughly."

"Oh my God."

The door closed behind Stewart and silence fell over the room, a silence Phil did not intend to break. His presence at the interrogation was not according to Hoyle and Stewart would have to go through the questions again once he had secured a lawyer for Byers.

"I didn't do it."

"So you've said."

"Don't you believe me?"

"I would be surprised if you admitted it."

"Of course I haven't. Because I didn't do it."

Silence.

"You're the brother of Professor Knight, aren't you?"

"That's right."

"Why are you here?"

"The university has retained me."

"Oh."

"Do you know my brother?"

"I know who he is. He's hard to miss."

Phil did not react. He did not encourage comments on Roger's girth. He himself was beginning to wonder if he really enjoyed being back in the saddle again, to the degree that he was. From the beginning, he had been quietly scandalized by the series of events meant to embarrass the university in the matter of its claim to its land. He might have felt differently if any real Native Americans were involved in the incidents. But it all had the look of radical chic, borrowed indignation, an exercise in political correctness. It dismayed him that anyone should want to bring the university into disrepute. It dismayed him more that the administration seemed to have no swift way of handling the charges. He had heard of the planned White Paper, not a bad idea, but by the time it was written, time would have passed and it might serve only to stir up what had died down.

The door opened and Jimmy beckoned him into the hall. "Wait for me," he said to Byers.

The busy hallway was a contrast to the isolation of the interrogation room. Jimmy waited for several officers to pass.

"I'm going to let him go."

Phil nodded. Jimmy must have been thinking how difficult it would be to get an indictment.

"The murderer has confessed."

"Bacon?"

Jimmy looked directly at him then, and it was difficult to decipher his expression.

"No. Professor Otto Ranke."

42

Professor Otto Ranke's confession that he had killed his former student Orion Plant electrified the campus. Roger Knight had been kept abreast of developments by Phil, and by Lieutenant Stewart's visits as well, but he had not felt any impulse to get involved, not after his inquiries had turned suspicion on Orion Plant. The investigation pursued all the available spoors, but Roger was a firm believer in the contingency of things and thought, but did not say, that the murderer could easily be someone utterly unconnected with what Jimmy and Phil were pursuing. Bacon had conveniently admitted to transporting the body, but his denial that he had killed Orion was plausible to Roger just because it seemed so implausible that he would go to such trouble to remove the body of a man he had not killed. As for Byers, the events had the requirements for a fictional plot, but seemed devoid of solid legal base. Roger's heart sank within him when Phil called to tell him of Otto Ranke's confession. In a way he would have hesitated to call intuition, Roger was immediately struck by the plausibility of the professor's confession. It might seem that Ranke had no compelling motivation for killing Orion, but Roger knew otherwise. Above all, he knew about Ranke's daughter, Laverne. He decided to go to Holy Cross House and talk with Father Carmody.

It was the first time he had used his golf cart since its role in transferring Orion Plant's body had become known. The police had finally returned it to him, but Roger had eschewed its use. When he came within sight of the library, he abruptly changed his mind. First he would have a chat with Whelan.

The news about Ranke brought back Whelan's stammer and for half a minute he could say nothing. Then his ease with Roger asserted itself.

"He confessed?"

"Yes."

"But why?"

"He says because he killed Orion."

"I meant, why would he kill him?"

"Revenge."

He explained it to the learned archivist, but Whelan was inexperienced in the ways of love, of man for woman, of parent for child. "The man was dropped by the university. He would have gone away."

"But he hadn't."

He realized that Whelan did not know all he knew. It took time away from more interesting topics to pass on to the archivist the twists and turns of the investigation into Orion Plant's death. Laying out in linear order the things that Orion had engineered to embarrass the university, the effort apparently accelerated by the expulsion Whelan had mentioned. On the fatal night, there had been a meeting and then Orion had set out to stage a solo raid on the worshipers at the grotto. He never got there, though his lifeless body might have been carried past the grotto as it was taken to where it was found.

"But none of that has anything to do with Professor Ranke. Surely he didn't take part in any of those things."

"His daughter did."

Whelan sat back. "The girl who worked downstairs."

"Laverne Ranke."

"She has the reputation of being strange."

"She and Orion were very close. I think it was assumed that marriage was in the offing, and then suddenly he married Marcia."

"She worked in the Huddle."

For an apparently dedicated bachelor, Whelan seemed well informed about unattached females on the campus.

"Leaving Laverne in the lurch."

"So."

"Recently they had renewed their relations. To Professor Ranke's disgust. If he learned of his daughter's involvement in Orion's silly pranks, well . . ."

"You really think he killed Orion Plant?"

It would have been so easy to say no. Roger wanted to say no. But from what he knew of Professor Ranke he could believe that the eminent historian would take strong measures against a man who threatened to ruin his daughter's life a second time.

"I don't believe it," Whelan said.

"I hope you're right."

But Whelan suddenly changed gears. "I better get busy gathering materials on this, for the archives."

"For *The Book of Kills*?"

"I hate puns." But it was the amateur compiler of the initial account of strange deaths at Notre Dame who peeved Whelan.

Roger left, and when he emerged from the elevator on the first floor he was surprised to see Laverne Ranke working at the check-out counter. She performed her task with chill efficiency — scanning the identification card into the computer, doing the same with the books, running their spines over a magnet that would deactivate them so they would not sound the alarm when the bearer left the library. She was pasting a slip into the back of a book when she noticed Roger. Her cold mask of a face broke into a grotesque smile and she waggled her fingers at him.

She could not know yet about her father. Roger had no inclination to be the bearer of such news. He waggled his fingers in answer and passed into the concourse of the library.

Outside, snow had begun to fall, driven at a slant by the north wind. Roger gathered his scarf more tightly around his neck. The action put him in mind of a noose. Professor Otto Ranke had put his own head into a noose. He would not include in his confession that he was doing this for his daughter. When that occurred to the investigators, it would prompt them to ask why he would do anything so drastic to protect Laverne. What had she done? Or what had Professor Ranke thought she'd done? Roger stood for a moment peering through the blinding snow. There was of course the straightforward explanation that Ranke gave. He had killed Orion because the man was a dangerous fool who had brought dishonor on his former department and on the university. That he had also trifled with Ranke's daughter only added fuel to the fire of his rage. It was quite possible that Otto Ranke had confessed to killing Orion Plant because in fact he had killed him.

But how must Mrs. Ranke be taking all this? Roger lowered his head and headed into the weather toward his golf cart. He would stop by the Ranke house to talk with Freda.

She looked out at him over the door chain with frightened eyes. He threw back the hood of his commodious jacket and she cried out with recognition.

"Professor Knight, come in, come in."

The house was warm as toast, but the absence of Otto was palpable. He was surprised to find her alone, but so she was. She took his coat and still holding it looked at him tragically. Suddenly, she threw herself in his arms and he tried to comfort her. She was babbling in the German dialect of her girlhood, but it was scarcely articulated sound. This was the wail of a woman crushed by events. She stepped back, her eyes aswim with tears, looked at his dripping coat and then, scolding herself, bore it away to the closet.

"He didn't even tell me what he was going to do. I received a phone call from a reporter and then I checked and it's true. He has gone mad."

"Does Laverne know?"

"Oh my God, the girl."

"Sit down, Freda. Sit down."

"What possessed him to say he killed that

terrible young man?"

"Who will believe him?"

"The police! They are holding him. What should I do?"

"My brother Philip is with him. In a moment I will call him and get news."

"You must take some schnapps." The suggestion was an order. She poured two small glasses with a deft twist of her wrist and brought one immediately to her lips. It was clear who needed the schnapps. Roger lifted his glass and sniffed it, he rolled the viscous liquid in the glass, and set it on the table. If charity demanded, he would drink it, but there was enmity between him and alcohol.

Freda sought the great therapy of talk. She gave a jumbled account of their dealings with Orion Plant. She said the name as if doing so were a confessable fault. How he had led poor Laverne on, and all of them, if the truth were known. That the young couple should marry seemed inevitable. Freda had only realized when Orion married another how much she disliked him. It had broken Laverne's spirits. Freda took the rest of her schnapps and looked speculatively at the other glass. He pushed it toward her.

"Then he came back. A married man, and he came calling on Laverne as if nothing had happened. How she welcomed him. Oh, the stupid stupid girl. But there is more, something worse."

"What?"

"Laverne . . ." Her eyes had been full of tears all along, but now they leaked from her eyes and ran down her Dresden china cheeks. "The stupid, stupid girl."

There is no easy way for a mother to communicate such a disgrace. Roger would have been hard pressed later to recall the exact words Freda had used. Some of them were German. But the message was clear. Laverne was with child. The father had to be Orion.

"Didn't she say?"

"She boasted of her condition. She has no shame."

"I wonder if Orion knew."

Freda didn't know. There was a sound of the lock of the front door turning, but Freda had put up the chain. She went to the door.

"Mother, let me in. Why have you chained the door?"

A moment later, Laverne came in. Her uncovered head was asparkle with melting snow, her cheeks were flushed, she looked momentarily beautiful. She stared quizzically at Roger Knight. Not half an hour before they had exchanged waves in the library. She turned to her mother.

"Is it true?"

"You've heard."

"I was told to come home, something had happened to Dad. Where is he?"

"In jail!"

Roger did not want to sit through another rendition of the story. Freda got his coat and kissed him wetly on the cheek, her lips sticky with schnapps. "Thank you for coming, Professor Knight. You are a good man."

Laverne gave him a small smug smile, a woman with a secret. Roger could imagine her boasting of her condition. He went out into the snow.

43

The reaction in the Main Building was ambiguous. The arrest of Bacon had seemed to write finis to the troubles that had been plaguing the university, but then Ballast brought word to the chancellor that the police had taken another graduate student in for questioning. Scott Byers. Anita Trafficant brought up his file, printed it out, and brought it in to the chancellor. He looked at her like a man who had just learned that his canceled execution was rescheduled for the morning. He studied the print-out. It meant nothing to him. Ballast took it and frowned over it.

"Did you ever hear of him?" he asked Anita.

"No."

She had heard the soap opera details of Byers's on-again, off-again relations with Marcia Younger Plant. "The life of the mind?" The chancellor hit his head. "And people complain about the behavior of our athletes." Another storm that had blown over.

"Maybe Byers is one of the band that kidnapped me." He looked around with a Lone Eagle expression. Anita felt something akin to compassion. Who does not magnify his own troubles? She went back to her adjoining office. It was there that she got the call from Maudit that Professor Otto Ranke had turned himself in and confessed to the murder of Orion Plant. Maudit wanted to know what the reaction of the administration was.

"You're making this up."

"So you haven't heard."

There was a lilt in his voice at the possibility. "Look, go tell the great man and then come back and describe it for me."

She hung up. After a moment's hesitation, she called the police and asked for Lieutenant Stewart. He was busy. She was giving the number he should call when she had a thought. "Is Philip Knight there?"

"Just a minute."

And in less than a minute Philip Knight was on the line.

"Is it true about Professor Ranke?"

"I'm afraid it is."

"Do they believe him?"

"He is very persuasive. And calm."

"He says he killed Orion Plant?"

At that moment Ballast passed her desk

292

and heard the question. He skidded to a halt. Anita ignored him.

"He couldn't have. Are they holding him?"

"He insists on it."

Philip Knight had to go, they were still going over Professor Ranke's story with him. Anita rose and, with Ballast at her heels, went into the chancellor. She felt like Captain Hornblower about to witness a flogging.

"Professor Ranke has confessed to the murder of Orion Plant."

"Otto Ranke? Nonsense."

Anita waited. He saw that the message was true. Ballast cried, "I'll get down there to represent our interests."

"Yes, yes. Can it be kept quiet?"

Ballast knew when to answer and when not to answer. He hurried off. The chancellor plunged his face in his hands. Anita withdrew, not wishing to see a grown man cry. Had he given any thought to poor Professor Ranke?

Her phone rang off the hook and she directed callers to public relations. Bartleby from that office called and asked what the hell was going on. She directed him to the police.

"They're saying that Professor Ranke has been arrested for murder."

"Actually, he confessed."

"And you didn't let me know?"

Bartleby managed to slam down his phone

before she could slam down hers. And then a moment of silence reigned. But in Anita's mind an old thought started up again. The jail was filling with people suspected of killing Orion Plant. Images of Harold rapidly replaced one another on the screen of her mind, mental MTV. Doubts she thought she had quelled came back with renewed force. After he admitted erasing his middle name from his file when he found it on her computer, he had gone on about his family. She had been almost surprised by the atavistic enthusiasm with which he spoke of his ancestors. The fact that they had lived here from the beginning obviously meant much to him. His job at the university, however humble, promised promotion, and it had reestablished the connection of his family with the university, after all these years. He talked of the Cruelles and the Youngers.

Younger. She called up Orion Plant's file, still in the database despite the fact that he had been dropped from the graduate school, despite the fact that he was now dead. Married? Yes. Spouse's name. Marcia Younger Plant. The Youngers had been one of the early families too. Marcia worked in the Huddle. Had that reestablished a link between her ancestors and Notre Dame? Anita had a sudden sense of a vast infrastructure beneath the present, a past all but unknown to those who occupied this land now. Had Marcia Younger's pride been similar to Harold's? Had she been behind her husband's mad campaign to prove this land had been gotten in a questionable manner?

Sandra Trepani, the toothy senator, called and asked if they could talk.

"So talk."

"Can I come there?"

"I guess so."

She blew in on the bad news she had just picked up, smiling like Bugs Bunny. She glanced at the closed door of the chancellor's office.

"How is he taking it?"

"I talked him out of hanging himself."

"He should have followed the advice of the senate."

"Which advice?"

"The open hearing."

Quinlan, his mind agog after hours of C-Span, had indeed proposed an open hearing, himself presiding, in which testimony would be given on the matters now contested concerning the title rights to the land on the shores of Saint Mary's and Saint Joseph's lakes. It would be televised, of course. Had he imagined himself bearing down on administrators and extracting incriminating admissions?

"How did they drive Ranke to do this? What do they have on him?"

"It obviously benefits the university to have a senior professor confess to murdering a graduate student."

But irony was wasted on Trepani.

"Quinlan has a new idea."

"Ah."

"He has already summoned the executive committee of the senate for an emergency meeting."

"Why aren't you there?"

She glanced at her watch. "I have time. I had hoped you would give me some sense of the line the administration will take."

"At the moment, they are disposed to let the law take its course."

"Sacrifice Ranke?"

"He has thrown himself on the altar."

That was better than Trepani had hoped for. She gathered up her things and tottered on her high-heeled snow boots. She urged Anita to call her with news of any developments.

"I can be summoned from the special session. Or you can leave a message on my home phone."

"If something comes up."

A little gloved hand grasped Anita's. It might have been the secret handclasp of the sisterhood.

When she left, Anita felt that the chancellor had been abandoned and was naked to his enemies. Ballast had gone downtown. He sat alone on his seat of power, none of his advisors about him. Anita asked if she should call someone to be with him.

"That is good of you."

"Meaning yes?"

He waved a weary hand. "No. I think not. I want to be alone for a time."

When she arrived home, Harold was waiting for her.

44

Bacon was retained in custody, pending bail. Although Ranke's confession freed him of the most serious charge, the fact that he had tampered with the scene of the crime and transported a dead body were cause enough to charge him. Not that Jimmy thought that anything would come of it, but the investigation into the death of Orion Plant had taken too many twists to accept any present simple solution. The fact was, he did not believe Ranke's confession, but then he didn't quite disbelieve it either.

"Too bad for the university," Kocinski said, in conference with Kreps the prosecutor. "But nice for us. People are complaining that we're giving Notre Dame special treatment."

"With three people from there under lock and key?" Kreps favored monosyllables so that the occasional iambic foot made his level tone seem almost musical.

"But not all of them are guilty. The professor is a godsend." Kocinski was demeaning himself in his effort to impress the prosecutor.

Kreps, after many lucrative years in the legal department of a local bank, had to the surprise of all his friends announced his candidacy for prosecutor. Since he had no previous political experience, he looked the picture of innocence next to his experienced and thus tainted opponent. But his opponent was a member of the party that had controlled the city for years, whose members would vote for a serial murderer if he had the party's nomination. Kreps launched his campaign by saying that one of his first acts would be to indict his opponent for malfeasance in office. Whereupon he began to tick off offenses the opponent had thought were known only to himself and his dark angel. Kreps was elected largely because people wondered if he would keep his promise. He did. It was a relief for the police not to have to rely on his predecessor, but Kreps always needed convincing that a legitimate case could be made, by which he meant one he could not lose. Jimmy was glad he would not have to persuade Kreps that Byers had done in Orion.

"What are we holding him for?" Kreps asked.

Kocinski looked at Jimmy.

"Adultery."

Kreps looked at Kocinski, but his eyes returned to Jimmy. "There is a statute on the books, but I don't think anyone has ever been prosecuted for adultery in this county."

"I want to hold him the maximum time without indicting him."

Kreps had read the account of Otto Ranke's confession. He turned now to that. "Why did he do this?"

"He's the man," Kocinski said. "He admits it."

Kreps narrowed his eyes. "I assume that the professor is no fool. Let us say we indict him and bring him to trial. This confession is our pièce de résistance. He repudiates it on the stand, says he made it for whatever reason, duress, a momentary madness. Where does that leave us?"

Jimmy liked Kreps. A man with a constant sense of impending disaster was someone you could work with. If he had any beef against the Knights, it was their conviction that some at least of life's mysteries could be definitively solved. But Phil was a good companion on the investigation and Roger from time to time chimed in with something surprising and useful.

"Roger asked if we had looked into Marcia Plant's relatives," Phil said.

"Does she have any? She was alone at the funeral."

"Just one of Roger's questions."

But the two men observed a moment of silence, as if to convince themselves they had taken the question seriously if it later proved significant, but Jimmy certainly didn't know what Roger was getting at. Nonetheless, he asked Donna de Laredo to check it out. She looked like a pair of glasses wearing a head, and spent the day hunched over her computer.

"What is the family name, sir?"

"I forget: They were married here, it should be on the license."

Donna had not asked how to do her job. She pursed her lips, then turned back to the completely rational world in which she dwelt, where everything was reducible to combinations of plus and minus, and all errors were human ones.

After Phil left, Jimmy closed his office door, leaned back in his chair, and with closed eyes wrote a draft of an interim report to be stored in the hard drive of his brain.

Item. Orion Plant, a graduate student of questionable talent, overstayed his welcome and was dropped from the doctoral program in which he had spent too many years.

Item. Plant had married a local girl,

301

Marcia whatever, dumping the daughter of Otto Ranke to do so.

Item. Laverne Ranke worked at the check-out desk in the Hesburgh Library, Marcia whatever worked in the Huddle. (Donna could find the name in her Notre Dame records as well.) Orion had not ventured far afield in his quest for female companionship. Laverne had taken her repudiation hard, dwindling noticeably; already a taciturn young lady, she had become all but autistic until Orion renewed his attentions, whereupon Marcia sought consolation with Scott Byers.

Item. Laverne had been recruited into Orion's mad campaign to embarrass the university, a campaign that intensified when his protector in the history program, Professor Ranke, perhaps in retaliation, had stopped defending Orion and he had been dismissed from graduate studies.

Item. When suspicion fell unequivocally on Orion, thanks to the inquiries of Roger Knight, and Orion was being sought, he had disappeared and his body was found near the Fatima Retreat House by Father James while feeding the ducks on a day when an unseasonal snow still lay upon the ground.

Item. A tire print found at the scene had led to a painstaking effort to match it with a university vehicle which had surprisingly ended with the discovery that the telltale tire was on Roger Knight's golf cart, the means of transportation of the oversize Huneker Professor of Catholic Studies.

Item. Russell Bacon during routine questioning suddenly blurted out that he had removed the body from the area of graduate student housing, using Roger's cart for the purpose, but denied having murdered Orion Plant. He neglected to say that he had come upon the body on the doorstep of the building in which he and his wife lived, one of the buildings that a few years before had been redesigned for married students, the buildings that had been built for this purpose near the toll road — Fertile Acres, as they were called — being filled to overflowing, with a long list of married applicants seeking a residence on campus. The assumption to that point had been that the body had been found near Roger Knight's golf cart, hoisted upon it, and driven into the night. This new information seemed to solve the puzzle as to why Bacon had gone to such trouble rather than simply sounding the alarm.

Item. An additional motive for the deed Bacon admitted to was that he had taken part in a meeting at Plant's in which Orion announced that he would undertake a solo act that would intensify the embarrassment of the university, namely, in Indian costume to break up a group saying the rosary at the grotto and reclaim the land for the natives from which it had been stolen.

Item. Laverne Ranke had also been present at the meeting. Ranke said that he had followed his daughter there, watched her leave the meeting, and then followed Orion Plant when he set off for the grotto. He caught up with him, seized the tomahawk, and brought it down savagely on his head. He left him for dead on the doorstep of what turned out to be the Bacon's building, Orion having sought refuge there when Ranke attacked him.

Item. The arrest of Scott Byers, and the

earlier one of Bacon, were thus rendered unjustified, at least so far as either of them being the murderer of Orion Plant was concerned.

Those were the pieces of the puzzle which, with Otto Ranke's confession, fell neatly into place. They either confirmed or in any case did not conflict with his statement that he had followed Laverne and, in the circumstances he described, killed his former student.

Professor Ranke sat comfortably through the many grillings to which he was subjected with the serenity of a seminar director whose main interest was to help his interlocutors establish the truth of what he said.

"You were outraged by the events designed to bring the university into disrepute?"

"How could I not be?"

"And you formed the theory that Orion Plant was at the bottom of these episodes?"

"I did."

"Why didn't you wait for justice to be done?"

"It is in order that justice be done that I have stepped forward."

"I refer to the time before Orion's death. You knew he was under suspicion and that it was only a matter of time, a short time, when he would be charged."

"I feared that he would escape your clutches."

"Flee?"

"No. Recent litigation, both internal and external, had shown that the university was at a disadvantage when a conflict arose between the university and a student."

Ranke reviewed for them the cases he had in mind. Internally, the plagiarism accusation against Bacon more than sufficed. The man was as guilty as sin, yet he was brazen enough to destroy the evidence that proved his guilt. He showed no more compunction for what he had done than Orion Plant.

"The accused must be presumed innocent, of course, but the fact is that the guilty are usually judged to be innocent."

There was more. Disgruntled faculty who had been denied tenure succeeded in having painstaking decisions reversed or extracting large amounts of money from the university. As for external cases, he referred his questioners to the way in which first the *Picayune* and then the other local paper had uncritically adopted the cause of those accusing the university of having illicitly procured title to the land on which it was built.

"Against this background, I had every reason to expect that Orion Plant would emerge exonerated and doubtless accorded the status

306

of hero in the matter. I could not abide that thought."

Ranke, while old, was a strong and healthy man. It did not strain the imagination that, fueled by a father's wrath, he might have overwhelmed Orion Plant and brought the tomahawk crashing down on his head.

"I do not, of course, intend that anything I have said should be taken as an excuse for the dreadful deed I performed. I acted in the full realization that I was killing another human being and must face the consequences of what I have done. That is why I came to you and told the whole story."

How tidy it all seemed. Yet Jimmy was not satisfied. Kocinski insisted that the arraignment be scheduled.

"The sooner we get an indictment, the sooner we will expunge the memory of those previous arrests."

Kreps was impressed by Stewart's reluctance to make haste in the matter. He adjourned the meeting and set an hour some days hence when he would meet again with those pursuing the investigation. He had clearly been impressed by Professor Ranke's description of the ambience in which the prosecution would go forward.

"I want no loose ends," he said.

"Such as?" Kocinski demanded, clearly annoyed by the prosecutor's postponement of the inevitable. But Kreps stood, and bowed them out. The meeting was over. Kocinski went off in a huff and Stewart returned to his office. There was a note from Donna de Laredo on his desk. "Marcia Plant's maiden name was Younger." Of course. He had known that. Must not tell Donna.

45

Professor Ranke received Roger with all the warm formality with which he would have received him in his office or at his home. He waited for Roger to get stabilized on one of the suddenly fragile looking chairs in the visiting room and then sat himself.

"We meet under tragic circumstances, Roger."

"I stopped to see Freda. You can imagine her condition."

A shadow of pain passed over the professorial brow. "The effect of this on her represents my deepest regret. But if 'twere done 'twere well 'twere done quickly. Why should I put off the evil day and wait for the police to work laboriously toward me?"

"Laverne is with her, of course."

"A great consolation," Ranke said, looking Roger in the eye.

Roger sought in vain for a way to bring up the matter of Ranke's embryonic grandson. Indirection seemed indicated. "She seemed radiant."

"Eventually Freda too will see that a great

weight has been lifted from the family. Unforgivable as my deed was, Freda will come to see that I acted, in my way, honorably."

"As a wronged father?"

"You know the whole sordid story."

"Of course the renewal of the relationship between your daughter and Orion must have been the last straw."

Ranke was permitted his pipe and he drew from it a great mouthful of smoke and then sent a series of neatly defined smoke rings toward the ceiling of the room.

"My testimony that I was acting in the name of a wronged university is not false. That a man who had failed to take advantage of the great opportunity offered him by this university should mount such a despicable attack on it was beyond bearing."

"But any loyal son of Notre Dame had equal motivation with you."

"I said it was not a falsehood that these outrages motivated me. I did not say they were my sole reason."

"Or your principal reason?"

In answer, Ranke sent another series of smoke rings upward.

"When did you learn of your daughter's condition?"

Ranke closed his eyes in pain. "There is no reason to make that more public than it already is." He opened his eyes. "I beg you not to make this known to the police."

"You were already sufficiently wronged as a father."

"Exactly. That a married man should take up again with a girl he had treated so cruelly is more than sufficient for a father to take action. Moreover, I had professional dealings with the scoundrel. He abused my constancy in defending him against legitimate doubts that he was not in fact hard at work on his dissertation. If that had been the case, my colleagues and the graduate school were justified in bending the rules. Besides, they would not have wanted to act contrary to the wishes of the director of the dissertation. When I withdrew my support, Orion's days as a graduate student were over."

"Did he ever threaten you?"

Professor Ranke smiled through the cloud bank he had created. "Ah. You are looking for extenuating reasons."

"If you felt your life was in danger. . . ."

"Perhaps something could be made of the situation created by my being chiefly responsible for his dismissal. But I cannot testify that he actually threatened me."

"Actually."

"Delete actually. I am ashamed of myself. No, I will not try to hide behind the shield of alleged self-defense. A preemptive strike, as we used to say during the Cold War."

And then, in what would have seemed incredible in the eyes of the uninitiated, the conversation turned to scholarly matters. Ranke wanted to know how Roger's seminar in Barbey D'Aurevilly was going.

"Roger, I see you as carrying on the work in which I have been humbly engaged. The writing of history is always an ineffectual effort against the forgetfulness of the past. You must continue to give such seminars."

"Did Orion ever talk to you about the records of Younger Real Estate?"

"No. Why do you ask?"

"A room in his home was full of these records. Clearly they had provided material for his campaign against the university."

"And who is Younger Real Estate?"

"Was. It was the business engaged in by Marcia Plant's ancestors. Dating back to the nineteenth century while Father Sorin was still alive. Of course, it was not called that from the beginning. But the original Younger dealt in land transactions."

"That is news to me."

"It was news to Whelan in the university archives as well."

"Have you had an opportunity to study these papers?"

"Only cursorily thus far."

"And you will go on doing so?"

"I shall try to persuade Marcia Plant to turn them over to the archives."

"Good. Good."

When Roger, after several attempts, rose to go, it might have been to terminate a conversation like so many others he'd had in the past with Otto Ranke.

"Freda will be well provided for," Ranke said.

"And Laverne?"

"Laverne of course."

What must be Otto Ranke's feelings at the realization that Orion Plant's child inhabited the womb of his daughter? Roger wondered. It was unlikely that Laverne's condition would remain secret. For one thing, Laverne herself was likely to announce to the world that she was pregnant with Orion's child. She had not behaved at all like a woman in disgrace.

46

Anita Trafficant had not shown up for work and did not answer her telephone at home, so Ballast offered the chancellor the use of his secretary. It did not escape his mind that Carole's permanent settlement at Anita's desk would have advantages to the university counsel. Carole's first loyalty would continue to be to himself, and then the blank spots in ongoing business that were kept from Ballast would be at his disposal. No cross lay heavier on his shoulders than to be informed of something he should have known but had not. Informants had a manner in such situations that strained Ballast's composure to the utmost. It was the essence of his professional outlook that he should be privy to everything and that he should hold in secret what was unknown to others. The delights of being in the know, in the inner ring, surpassed all other earthly joys.

He shook these thoughts away with difficulty. It was silly to think that the hitherto Iron Woman of the Main Building was not subject to the ills men — and women (even in his private reveries, Ballast was careful to use inclusive language) — were heir to.

"I could phone Harold," Carole said, looking at him over the tops of her glasses.

"Harold?"

"There seems to be something going on between them."

Here was a case in point. His own secretary knew things he did not. Ballast had no idea who Harold might be.

"He works in the computing center."

"On campus?"

"Yes."

"Find out if he is in. Discreetly."

He went into the chancellor's office, where the topic of discussion was whether or not to fire Otto Ranke. The chancellor followed the exchange among his advisors with a pained expression.

"I studied with him as a student."

"There is no guilt by association," Ballast said, plunging into the discussion.

At Anita Trafficant's desk, Carole was looking up the number of the computer center when her phone rang. She picked it up and managed to remember to say "Chancellor's office."

"Anita? You can imagine our fury. We will not stand by and allow them to railroad an esteemed colleague into prison on trumped-up charges."

"Who is speaking, please?"

A long silence ensued. "Who am I speaking to?"

"This is the chancellor's office."

"I want to speak to Anita Trafficant."

"She hasn't come in today."

The phone went dead. Honestly. Carole had found the number of the computing center. She dialed it and asked for Harold.

The phone was put down and minutes later the voice that had answered said, "He must be out on a job."

"This is the chancellor's office."

"Anita?" The voice turned pleasant.

"No. I am sitting in for her today. I must locate Harold."

"I'll try to reach him."

At her own desk in the university counsel's suite, Carole would have had a dozen tasks to do. But at this strange desk, she sat in helpless inactivity. She looked at the closed door of the chancellor's office. She opened and closed drawers. She got up and checked the coffee, but there was still three-quarters of a pot. She poured a cup and took it to her desk. She turned to the computer, brought up the word processing program, and began to write a nonsense memo to herself. Of course she would neither store it nor print it out, but she had to be doing something. She summarized what had happened since Mr. Ballast had told her to take over for the absent Miss Trafficant. That was soon done.

Carole had no ambitions beyond the position she now held. She had been a legal secretary and enjoyed the pointless precision of the documents she typed. Mr. Ballast was a demanding boss, largely because of his frenetic jumping from problem to problem, many of them imaginary. Some, of course, were not. Carole had to suppress her sympathy with those with a grievance against the university, but Mr. Ballast relished his role of advocate for and defender of the university, no matter what. Of course, that was the appropriate attitude of the university counsel; she wasn't criticizing him, not even in the privacy of her own mind. Loyalty came easily to her. Still, it was unnerving to see the relentless way Mr. Ballast proceeded against those who had been denied tenure and had the gall to take the university to court.

Sufficient time had gone by to justify another call to the computing center.

"He might not have come in today," she was told when she asked again about Harold. "I called his house but he doesn't answer."

Carole hung up the phone, but her hand

still lay upon it. She was not a prurient woman, but she had noticed Anita and Harold together. Carole was married to a good man and had a son for whom she feared. She read jumbo novels with guilty pleasure, she had listened to talk shows on television, she had secondhand knowledge of the ways of the world. She picked up the phone and dialed Anita's apartment.

The ringing went on and on, unanswered. Carole imagined a couple, impervious to that ringing, wrapped in one another's illict arms. Such things happened. One heard of them every day. Finally she hung up the phone, feeling like the audio version of a Peeping Tom. She did not relish reporting the results of her efforts to Mr. Ballast, but of course she must do so.

It was the first thing he asked when he emerged from the chancellor's office in company with others who had been involved in the meeting.

"He apparently hasn't come in today."

"Were you able to reach Anita?"

"Her phone is not answered."

"Call Harold."

"He doesn't answer either."

"Well, well." Mr. Ballast looked to see the reaction of the others. "I'm worried about her. Someone ought to check. After what has been happening on this campus . . ." He left the sentence unfinished. He had an inspiration. "Get hold of Philip Knight and ask him to check out Anita's apartment."

47

Laverne Ranke came stumbling back into the library, which she had just left when her shift ended and evening had fallen, with the story that she had been attacked beside the reflecting pool. The reaction was mixed. Laverne's long history of aloof reticence now made her coworkers dubious. Her new cloth car coat was covered with snow, but there were no visible signs of physical harm.

"She probably slipped," said an unsympathetic voice.

Laverne broke into tears, the shock with which she had stumbled back inside gone. "My baby," she cried, placing the spread fingers of a pianist on her middle. "My baby."

And so the news had come out. A sudden sisterly solidarity formed among her fellow librarians, and Laverne was taken away, half carried, to the area behind the check-out desk where she was consoled and fussed over by women aroused by a condition that might be any one of theirs. Laverne's unmarried state was, at least for the nonce, forgotten.

That a daughter of the confessed murderer

of Orion Plant claimed to have been attacked beside the reflecting pool of the library drew different reactions elsewhere.

"The next thing we know Freda will claim to have been raped in her home."

"It runs in the family."

There was indeed something of the supererogatory in Laverne's allegation. Campus security checked the spot where the attack had allegedly occurred and found only a peaceful scene with what might have been a snow angel described in the newly fallen snow. It was soon received opinion that Laverne had faked the attack in order to have an occasion to announce her condition to the world.

Roger Knight heard of Laverne after Phil had responded to a request from the university counsel. He recalled his unspoken surmise when he was visiting Professor Ranke in the county jail. Laverne would be the one to make her condition public. And so she had. Roger shared the general skepticism about an attack being made on her person. He had already telephoned Marcia Plant and asked to see her. She would be home all night, she said. Not a warm welcome, but then he had hardly expected one.

After he got his golf cart unplugged from the recharging cable, he sat behind the wheel enjoying the sight of the snow drifting past a lamp some yards away. It might have been falling to cover with its innocence the astounding events that had been rocking the campus. When he pulled away, he decided to make a long detour past the place where Laverne claimed she had been attacked. He circled the area, which had been trampled by the feet of campus security and bumped over something hidden in the snow. Ignoring whatever it was was the preferable option, but he knew that he would later wonder what it had been. He unbuckled himself and got himself onto his feet. With the side of his boot he cleared away the snow. Then he stooped to pick up the tomahawk.

He managed to get it into one of the massive side pockets of his hooded jacket, stuffed the cloth with which he had wiped the snow off the seat into the same pocket, and continued on his way to the Plant residence.

Marcia Plant had the look of a young woman just realizing that she was all alone in the world. Her husband was dead. His eager replacement, Scott Byers, had been arrested by the police and, she suspected, would emerge from confinement with his ardor considerably cooled. She looked very much like bad luck to any eligible young man. In the circumstances, she seemed delighted to find

Roger Knight at her door and urged him to come in out of the snow. Roger stamped his boots on the stoop and entered, beginning the process of freeing himself from his outer garment, a hooded coat the athletic department had presented him with, a size far beyond XXL.

"Thirty," he remarked at the sight of the label. "Roman numerals."

"My age."

"I would never have guessed it." This was fact, not flattery. Roger had nothing of Philip's ability to guess the age of females.

"People say I'm still young, but thirty is old."

She hung his coat on a peg next to another dripping garment. The overshoes on the floor beneath had left fresh little puddles around them.

"Some people complain of snow. I've never understood that. It is beautiful outside."

She made a face. "You can have it."

He launched into his reason for coming. He had heard of the room set aside for the records of Younger Real Estate.

"Orion worked there. The records had been in storage, but Orion persuaded my mother to let him bring them here. He spent hours and hours up there."

"Your mother."

"She's in California with my brother. Maybe I'll go out there and begin a new life."

When Roger said nothing, she went on.

"You wonder why they didn't come back when all these things happened. Orion and my mother didn't get along. He was pretty pushy, just taking over the house as if it was ours, not my mother's. She got fed up and decided to go to California."

"And your father?"

"He's dead." The way the information was given surprised Roger, but she went on to say she had been a child when he died. "My memories of him are all blurred now. Of course, there are photographs."

"But your mother kept the records of the family business."

Marcia nodded. "But she resented having to pay rental for storing them. Orion never guessed that was her reason for agreeing that he should move them here."

"Why did he do that, I wonder."

"He had gone out there and poked around in the boxes. He got quite excited about it."

"Well, he was an historian."

"He wanted to be one, anyway. They threw him out of the university, you know."

"Yes. Professor Ranke told me."

An angry expression flickered on her face and was replaced by a look of wonder. "Imagine him just confessing like that."

"As a Catholic he's used to confessing."

"I suppose. I'm not a Catholic."

"The Youngers weren't Catholic?"

"Way back when, they were. My father had been baptized, but I guess it didn't take."

"Would you have had your children baptized?"

She looked at him. "We never had any." And then suddenly she was crying. "I wanted kids. I wanted to quit work and settle down to being a housewife and mother. Women who haven't worked or have cushy jobs say they don't want that, but I don't believe them. All my friends want a husband who earns the money while they raise the kids and take care of the house. I love to cook." She sobbed as if some impossibly attractive dream had receded beyond her grasp. "He didn't want kids."

"Orion?"

"That's what he said anyway."

"And now Laverne Ranke is pregnant."

"Who told you that?"

"She hasn't kept it a secret."

"But she isn't even showing."

"She blurted it out not long ago, when she escaped back into the library."

"That's her all over. What a terrible woman."

"You might have harmed the child. Orion's child."

She looked at him blankly.

"Excuse me for a moment." Roger levered himself to his feet and went to where she had hung his jacket. He took the tomahawk from the pocket and brought it back into the living room. "I found this."

She didn't quite recoil at the sight of the tomahawk, but she pressed back into her chair.

"It was covered with snow. If I hadn't found it, someone else would have."

"I don't know what you're talking about."

"You can't just hold it in, Marcia. Eventually, you'll go crazy thinking about it, or explode."

"You think I attacked Laverne?"

"How bitter it must have been to know Orion had gotten her with child when he refused to have children with his own wife."

"Oh, she seduced him. After all, he was only a man. Even a woman without looks can be attractive in certain situations."

"Did Orion tell you Laverne was pregnant?"

"Yes! The bastard. All that about waiting, we couldn't afford a family, not yet. There would be plenty of time later." She pounded her hand on the arm of her chair. "And then he stood right there, puffing up his chest like the cock of the walk, saying there was something I should know. Maybe he thought he was sterile or something. He was so *proud*. Did he expect me to congratulate him?"

"You were angry."

"Angry. I could have killed him."

"And you did."

She just let it go. She was still remembering her triumphant husband telling her another woman was carrying his child.

"When did he tell you?"

"That night. Before the others got here."

"And you sat through the meeting hating him."

"And her. She was here too."

"But she left with the others. And then Orion left. Did he know you were following him?"

"You think you're so smart, don't you?"

"I think it wasn't very smart of you to kill your husband, Marcia. I think you know that too. How you must have been suffering."

"If I did, it was his fault."

"It must be awful to be betrayed by your own husband."

The tears came again, self-pitying tears. The tears of a woman wronged who had tried to right that wrong and only made things infinitely worse.

"Thank God you didn't harm Laverne."

"I hope she loses her baby."

"Is that what you were trying to do?"

"I don't know! I had to do something. After all she had done. Orion was bad enough. You say he betrayed me and I suppose he did, but that didn't surprise me. Men do things like that."

"So do women."

"That's different."

He was tempted to tell her of those who had suffered for what she had done — of Carlotta's husband still in jail, of Scott Byers taken away for questioning, of Professor Otto Ranke. But he knew that would be a blind alley.

"You must have been surprised when the body was found where it was."

"I couldn't believe it. Why would Russell Bacon do such a thing?"

"To get the body off his doorstep."

"Orion nearly got to their doorbell." She stopped. "Would I have struck him if he hadn't tried to get help? He was going to get the Bacons on his side, they would all be against me. So I did it."

"Killed him."

"I struck him. I didn't mean to kill him."

A silence developed and Roger Knight sat looking at her. Perhaps she hadn't meant to kill Orion. That was between her and God.

"I think I should make a phone call."

It was a moment when she could have gotten hold of herself, denied everything, chased him from the house. But she nodded and Roger went to the phone.

EPILOGUE

Marcia Plant repeated her story when she was taken downtown, and afterward Lieutenant Stewart told Roger that this was absolutely the last confession of the murder of Orion Plant he wished to receive. Phil could not be located to hear this latest twist in the investigation so Stewart offered Roger a ride back to the campus.

"Father Carmody is coming for dinner tonight. Why don't you join us?"

"As one who has sampled your cooking, I accept."

"We'll start with cannelloni, go on to veal Parmesan with a salad of which I am justly proud, and end with spumoni."

"Is that a wine?"

"The wine will be a Chianti."

"My cup runneth over."

"If you like."

Stewart hovered in the kitchen, telling him of Professor Ranke's reaction when he was given the news he could go. "After all, we had nothing but his say-so for everything he said."

"The same can be said of Marcia Plant."

"Maybe not."

"How so?"

"The lab finally found a clear set of prints on the tomahawk. I mean the one found with the body."

"And?"

"We shall see."

Stewart did not act like a man who doubted the outcome of the match with Marcia's prints.

"A case is always difficult when you have so many people with good reason to have done the deed."

"And Bacon and Byers?"

"Byers has been released. Kreps is still deciding about Bacon."

"For moving the body?"

"It is an offense."

"What was your recommendation?"

"Send him home to his wife. I hope he never realizes that if she hadn't shrieked he would very likely have kept his own mouth shut."

"That is a lot to ask, in the circumstances."

"Kocinski is beside himself. I hope he likes the company."

"You're becoming a wit."

Stewart had been watching Roger roll the cannelloni with close attention. Now it was the turn of the veal.

"You have the stature of a chef."

"You would be surprised how many of the great chefs are thin as a rail. Many of them have bad stomachs and can only appreciate the results of their labors vicariously."

Father Carmody arrived, listened to the story of Marcia's confession, and then put it aside. "I am very uneasy about Saturday's game."

The game would be played far off, under the sun, in hostile territory. Of course the game would be on national television.

"I find a televised game far harder on my nerves. The camera is almost always focused on the action. In the stadium there are distractions, somehow the tension is less. Where is Philip?"

Roger had thought to call Ballast with the turn of events and had been told that Phil was performing a service for the university.

"What service?"

"I suppose I can tell you," Ballast said. "The chancellor's secretary is missing."

"Oh no."

"Nor can we locate her good friend who works in the computing center."

Roger brought this grim news back to his guests. Father Carmody perked up.

"What is her name?"

"Trafficant. Anita Trafficant."

"Why, I married her to a man named Harold Ivray in the Holy Cross chapel this afternoon. They were unwilling to wait until they could schedule the ceremony at Sacred Heart or the log chapel, they had a license, so of course I was happy to oblige them."

He raised his glass and Stewart raised his and they drank a before-dinner libation to the happy couple.

"Odd middle name the groom has. Cruelle."

"The name of the nineteenth-century serial murderer. Whelan has entered it all in *The Book of Kills*. It was one of the items Orion Plant had turned up in the course of his research."

"Why don't people concentrate on the great things that have happened here?" Father Carmody grumbled.

"Most do, Father. Most do. Professor Otto Ranke, for one."

At the mention of the name, Father Carmody made a face. "And I always thought he was a sensible man."

It was nearly seven when Phil came in, a grim expression on his face. "I'm afraid it isn't over. There are two more people missing."

333

"Anita Trafficant and Harold Ivray."

Phil stopped in the process of unwrapping himself. "How do you know that?"

Father Carmody then told him of the wedding he had officiated at in the chapel of Holy Cross House that afternoon. Phil just stared. He was in an appropriately stunned mood to receive the story of Marcia Plant's confession.

"Who will be next?" he asked.

"No one," Stewart assured him, watching Roger slide the cannelloni into the oven. "The contest is closed."

When Roger stopped by the Ranke home several days later, he found the returned professor getting the treatment his sisters must have accorded Lazarus after the first excitement of his emergence from the tomb was over. He sat in his great leather arm chair in his study, fussed over and tended to by his subservient wife. Schnapps was called for and schnapps was brought, but Freda did not join them.

"I never drink schnapps," she said, avoiding Roger's eyes.

Otto Ranke puffed on his pipe and accorded her a deeply affectionate look. The Rankes had been through the fire and, tried and tested, could face their remaining days in peace. Laverne had proved amenable to the suggestion that she go for what Ranke called her confinement to relatives in the East who were under the impression that she had lost her husband tragically.

"I have submitted my resignation, Roger. My last years will be devoted to my own work. I was offered an office in Flanner, but I refused. Instead, I have been given work space in the Maritain Center and shall work there and here. I must be near the sources, and where better than actually in the library?"

"And what will you work on?"

"I have three projects."

"Tell me."

"First, I will prepare a second and expanded edition of my book on great authors who have lectured at Notre Dame. The list has lengthened considerably since the book appeared, and I attended the lectures of all those I will add. Second, I will write a monograph on Father Petit, the heroic priest who accompanied the Indians who were displaced from here to the southwest. Many did not make it to their destination, including Father Petit."

"The influence of Orion Plant."

"There is more. If I live, I intend to complete the research Orion had scarcely begun that would have been his dissertation. I was reluctant at the time to give the topic to a tyro, and of course he grew bored with it."

"A tragic young man."

"I grieve for his wife. I have some intimation of what she is now going through."

"Of course. With the difference that she is guilty."

Professor Otto Ranke said nothing, just puffed on his pipe.

"You told a very convincing story."

"It was true."

"But, professor . . ."

Ranke held up his hand. "Did you think I could invent so many details? I did follow Laverne that night and stood in the snow outside the Plant residence. Eventually they emerged, but I noticed Plant was not in the group. I waited until he came out. I followed him."

"Why?"

"I intended to kill him."

Roger looked at his old friend, stupefied.

"To my chagrin, his wife then came out of the house and went after him. I crept along in pursuit, awaiting my opportunity. That is why I was a witness to what actually happened. As I watched, I confess I felt a deep satisfaction, not horror. She was doing what I feared Laverne might do. He had put my daughter in a most embarrassing condition, and then was through with her. A woman scorned . . ."

But the scorned woman who had struck Orion Plant was his wife.

"Then why did you confess?"

"In expiation for the ignoble way I felt when I watched a man killed. And to preserve a wife from the consequences of her deed."

The fire crackled, Otto Ranke lifted his glass of schnapps. Roger lifted the glass that Freda had insisted on pouring for him and made as if to drink. The aroma of the drink cleared his nasal passages.

"You could be called as a witness in the trial."

"Pray God it will not come to that." He looked at Roger. "Only two persons know that I was essentially telling the truth when I confessed. I will willingly confess no more."

After a long silence, Roger remembered an old school boy's gesture. He locked his lips and threw away the key.

The employees of Thorndike Press hope you have enjoyed this Large Print book. All our Large Print titles are designed for easy reading, and all our books are made to last. Other Thorndike Press Large Print books are available at your library, through selected bookstores, or directly from the publishers.

For more information about titles, please call:

(800) 223-1244
(800) 223-6121

To share your comments, please write:

Publisher
Thorndike Press
295 Kennedy Memorial Drive
Waterville, ME 04901